KATANA™
at SUPER HERO
HIGH

KATANA™
at SUPER HERO HIGH

By Lisa Yee

Random House 🏠 New York

PROLOGUE

"**C**'mon, Supers, let's get this party started," Harley Quinn cheered. Her blond pigtails bobbed up and down each time she landed a triple backflip. This was pretty amazing, considering she had a large mallet in one hand and her ever-present video camera in the other.

Harley pivoted on her landing and then focused the camera on Batgirl, Super Hero High's latest recipient of the Hero of the Month award. With so many of the universe's top super students at Super Hero High, this was one of the highest honors a teen could be awarded.

"I'd like to wait for Katana," Batgirl said, glancing at her watch. She adjusted the yellow Utility Belt she always wore around her waist. One never knew when they might need a laser screwdriver to adjust Cyborg's internal circuitry, a Batarang to thwart a criminal, or a Net Gun to pin an evil mutant against a wall.

"Well, Batgirl, it is your party," said the girl with the big *S* on her shirt. "Oops!"

"Watch out!" Cheetah warned everyone when Supergirl tripped on her own shoelaces—a not-uncommon occurrence for the girl who was quite possibly the most powerful being on Earth. Supergirl stumbled into Raven, who knocked into Frost, who almost fell over as Star Sapphire nimbly stepped aside and smiled as she adjusted the purple power ring on her finger as though nothing had happened.

Supergirl recovered and gracefully floated into a standing position. Her cheeks turned pink, and she smiled meekly as she made sure Raven and Frost were okay. The girls rolled their eyes good-naturedly. Luckily, Supergirl had gained more control over her powers during her time at Super Hero High, and her acts of random clumsiness were growing less frequent.

Meanwhile, Wonder Woman and Bumblebee were at the table arranging the black paper plates and yellow cups into a Batgirl logo . . . though it looked more like a lumpy kitten than a bat. "I wish Katana were here," Wonder Woman said. "She's so much better at this than we are."

"Where's the cake?" Big Barda asked as she barged into Batgirl's room, aka the Bat-Bunker. Each super hero had her own dorm room, with a shared living space in the middle of each quad. However, Batgirl had turned her room into a dark high-tech headquarters.

"Someone said there would be cake!" Barda said, looking at the empty plates. "Am I too late? Cake is my favorite food—well, after mashed potatoes, of course."

"Katana is picking up the cake from the Capes and Cowls Café," Wonder Woman said. "I'll go see if she needs help." She handed her paper cups to Bumblebee. "Be right back!"

In less time than it took for Bumblebee to finish the Batgirl logo, Wonder Woman had flown to Capes & Cowls, stopping on the way to use her Lasso of Truth to corral a trio of tricksters who were trying to hijack an ice cream truck.

"Hey, Steve!" Wonder Woman called. She pushed her thick black hair away from her face and adjusted her golden tiara with the red star emblazoned on the front.

As always, the Capes & Cowls Café was bustling. A lanky boy with a pencil tucked behind his ear blushed. This happened whenever Wonder Woman was around.

"Did she like it?" he asked.

"Like what?" Wonder Woman said as she shook his hand vigorously, not wanting to let go. Though his grip was not as strong as hers, she liked the way his head bobbed up and down. It was as if he were agreeing with her over and over again.

"Did Batgirl like the cake I made for her?" Steve said, flexing his hand until he had feeling in his fingers again. When Wonder Woman blinked blankly at him, he elaborated. "Seven layers? Purple and black buttercream frosting with lemon sugar piping? Big yellow Batgirl logo on the top? Katana did deliver it, right?"

"Katana was here and left?" Wonder Woman asked.

A look of concern crossed Steve's face as he replied, "She left over an hour ago and said she was heading straight back to Super Hero High. Katana said she didn't want to be late to the party, and we all know how punctual she always—"

Before Steve could finish his sentence, Wonder Woman was gone.

Back at the party, everyone gathered around Wonder Woman. "I don't know how to say this," she began, "but . . ."

"But what?" Supergirl pressed.

"Katana," Wonder Woman went on. "Steve said she picked up the cake over an hour ago and was heading right back here!"

Batgirl gasped. Harley was speechless. Even Cheetah looked worried. Finally, Bumblebee stated the obvious.

"This is totally unlike her," she said. "Katana is never late. Something must be terribly wrong!"

PART ONE

There was a party, all right. What was supposed to be a celebration party for Batgirl quickly turned into a search party.

Katana was missing! This was big. Of all the Supers, Katana had a reputation for being on time for everything. It was not unheard of for Katana to be extra early. But late? Never! Ever! Never ever!

Batgirl sat at the controls of her elaborate computer system in the Bat-Bunker while the others looked on. "I'm going to try to get a lock on her location," she explained as she addressed the keyboard with the speed, precision, and grace of a master pianist. Instantly, computer screens glowed blue, and images of the school grounds and the surrounding area appeared.

By then, the Bat-Bunker was crowded with concerned students. News traveled fast at Super Hero High, and they were famous for banding together when one of their own was in danger.

"Junior Detective Society, reporting!" Hawkgirl announced. In a nanosecond, The Flash was at her side, along with new member Poison Ivy, who was clutching an oversized basket of gorgeous tulips, daisies, and roses. She had been in charge of the flowers for the party and, after delivering the first batch, had left to get more. Half of her red hair was festooned with daisies. When she heard about Katana, Ivy had raced over without a thought to fixing the other half.

Batgirl nodded to her fellow detectives, glad for their assistance. They were known for cracking mysteries that ranged from who had eaten the last chocolate tart (Beast Boy) to knowing where an evil villain resided (the planet Xolnar). Just recently, the Junior Detective Society had helped Batgirl identify and capture the Calculator, a teen tech villain who sought to bring down the World Wide Web and control the world.

Instantly, the Junior Detective Society began interviewing everyone who might have a clue about Katana's whereabouts. The room was buzzing with theories, rumors, and an abundance of false leads.

"She probably dropped the cake and is too embarrassed to admit it," Cheetah said to The Flash.

"Maybe she was kidnapped by Croc," Big Barda told Poison Ivy as she swung her Mega Rod around, causing several Supers to duck or leap. "I heard he's on the loose again."

"It's possible she got sidetracked at the Metropolis Art Museum," Arrowette said to Hawkgirl. "They have a new Art of Archery exhibit."

"She's here," Miss Martian said so softly that only Supergirl could hear. "Katana is close."

"Where?" Supergirl asked. "Everyone, please! Miss Martian has detected something."

All talking stopped as Supers pressed in around the shy green alien from Mars. Supergirl could see Miss Martian starting to turn invisible, as she was apt to do when embarrassed, which was most of the time.

"Stay with us," Supergirl pleaded. "We need you! What do you know?"

Miss Martian shut her eyes to block out everyone who was staring at her. Though she had the ability to read minds, Miss Martian was never comfortable with the attention it brought her.

Batgirl took Miss Martian's hand and gently squeezed it. "It's okay," she assured her friend. "Pretend we're not here. Think about Katana."

Wonder Woman observed everyone looking at Miss

Martian, who had started fading again. "Please clear the room!" Wonder Woman yelled. "Let's give Miss Martian some space."

As teens began walking, flying, and tumbling out of the Bat-Bunker, Miss Martian began to appear again. Her forehead was furrowed as she concentrated. "I'm getting a signal from Katana," she said. "But it's weak."

Batgirl heaved a sigh of relief. "She's alive!" she said, stating what everyone else had been hoping. In this business of being a super hero, danger often lurked. Lives were saved, but lives were also often in jeopardy.

"Katana is in the building," Miss Martian added. Her delicate features were scrunched up as she tried to concentrate.

Batgirl leaned forward so that they were face to face. "Miss Martian," she said patiently, "are you getting a message? What can you tell us?"

"It doesn't make sense," Miss Martian said, shaking her head. "She's near, but she's far. Is she underneath us?" Suddenly, Miss Martian's eyes flew open. She began to tremble. "Katana's in danger!"

Batgirl gasped. "Underneath us? It must be the secret tunnels!"

"The what?" Supergirl asked as she flew in nervous circles around the room.

"I thought they were just an old Super Hero High urban legend," Poison Ivy said quizzically.

"Sometimes legends are based on fact," Wonder Woman noted. "Batgirl, since you have some knowledge of the tunnels, you look for Katana below. I'll round up the other Junior Detective Society members and go back to Capes and Cowls and try to see if I can come up with more clues."

"Sounds like a great plan," Batgirl said. But Wonder Woman had already left.

As the rest of the Supers began to fan out, four remained. Batgirl turned around to discover Miss Martian looking exhausted. Supergirl gave the green girl a warm smile and a hug, careful not to crush her. Poison Ivy handed her a flower.

Batgirl got on her computer and began referencing maps of catacombs and strange winding pathways. Using a special Bat-program, she was able to merge the documents; then she hit "Save" and downloaded the compilation onto her wrist computer.

"I'm trying to access the Metropolis building-code files. They go back over a hundred years, but only some of them have been digitized," Batgirl explained. "I can get us underground, but, Miss Martian, I'm going to need your help to find Katana. Are you up for this?"

Everyone stared at Miss Martian, whose green-skinned cheeks were now as red as her hair. Batgirl couldn't tell if she was scared, excited, or, more likely, both. "It's okay," Supergirl assured her. "We're all in this together."

Poison Ivy handed her a hybrid orange-rose blossom to "make you feel better." Miss Martian breathed its fragrant scent. "Okay," she said with quiet determination. "I'm ready."

"Let's go get Katana!" Supergirl said, already out the door and halfway down the hall.

"Hello?" Batgirl called after her.

"Hello!" Supergirl answered.

"You're going in the wrong direction," Batgirl pointed out.

"Oops! Maybe you should take the lead on this," Supergirl suggested.

"And Miss Martian, too," Batgirl reminded everyone. "We can't do it without her!"

"Should we tell Principal Waller?" Poison Ivy asked.

"*No,*" Miss Martian said with more force than usual.

Everyone froze.

"No," she said again, turning to her friends. She looked scared. "We have to hurry. There's no time to waste!"

CHAPTER 2

The map led the search party through the library, down the corridor, past Beast Boy's messy room, around Ivy's organic garden, over Mr. Lucius Fox's Weaponomics blast test zone, and back inside.

The rescue team of Batgirl, Supergirl, Poison Ivy, and Miss Martian stared at the small brown door near the cafeteria. It had been there forever, yet no one had ever really taken the time to notice. Most assumed it was where Parasite, the janitor, kept his cleaning supplies. There was a handwritten sign on the door in his distinctive scrawl.

> KEEP OUT. OR ELSE.
> THAT MEANS YOU. I AM SERIOUS.

Supergirl reached for the doorknob, prepared to rip the door off its hinges if necessary. However, the knob turned easily and the door swung open, making a small creaking sound. Everyone hesitated for a heartbeat before following Batgirl as she plunged into the darkness.

Always prepared, Batgirl lit up the maze of tunnels with her B.A.T.-light. Still, the light could not shine everywhere. It was cold and damp, and in spots water dripped from the low ceilings. The tunnels smelled like the bad parts of the beach.

With Batgirl at the front, Miss Martian at her side, the Supers weaved through tunnels and caverns. They hit so many dead ends that Poison Ivy began leaving a trail of petals so they could find their way back.

"A long time ago these tunnels were used to travel in and out of Metropolis unnoticed," Batgirl said. "Some evidence shows that they were once used as aqueducts to get to the ocean, and other evidence suggests that Supers and spies, and the government, used these passageways to hide secrets, treasures, and even people."

"This place is creepy!" Ivy declared as they forged onward. "There are so many doors and tunnels leading in every direction! I'm not so sure I want to know what's down here." She was staring at yet another door that was bolted shut.

The group paused as Batgirl asked Miss Martian, "Can you sense any thoughts from Katana in there?" They had been stopping at each door as Supergirl used her X-ray vision and Miss Martian tried to detect someone or something. So far, all the rooms had been empty.

Miss Martian shook her head. "I'm not picking up a signal anymore," she said. Her voice was filled with worry.

"Do you hear that?" Supergirl asked, cocking her head.

"I don't hear anything," Batgirl said.

Poison Ivy shook her head. "Me neither."

"I must be imagining things," Supergirl said. "For a moment I thought I heard a humming sound. A weird, creepy buzz like an out-of-tune radio."

"Supergirl, can you see what's on the other side of this door?" Batgirl asked, bringing her back to the task at hand.

All watched as Supergirl got into position and focused using her X-ray vision. "Let's break the door down," she said, not waiting for approval or help. "This room looks like it's full of clues!"

With ease, she lifted the worn wooden door off its hinges and leaned it against the wall. The Supers stood stunned at what lay before them. It was like a museum! There were shelves of memorabilia, old super hero costumes, a cache of ancient weapons, and grainy photos of some of their teachers when they were students at Super Hero High. A giant velvet painting of Crazy Quilt in a snazzy multicolored leisure suit was propped up against a pile of dusty capes with the initials *RT* on them.

"They must have belonged to Red Tornado," Supergirl said, talking about their flight instructor.

As the girls looked through the crates and boxes, Supergirl called out, "What are *you* doing here?"

Everyone faced the door.

"What's going on?" Beast Boy asked. He was munching on a piece of cake and humming a Pop 40 tune.

"Purple and black!" Batgirl shouted, staring at the frosting on his face.

"That's the cake Katana picked up from Capes and Cowls," Poison Ivy yelled, pointing to what Beast Boy was holding.

"Beast Boy! Where did you get that?" Supergirl demanded.

"Hey! Whoa, whoa, whoa," he said, pushing them away. "Get your own cake. There's plenty for everyone!"

"This is serious," Batgirl said. "Katana picked up my celebration cake from Steve Trevor before she went missing. We think she might be in danger."

Beast Boy looked stricken. "I didn't know!" he insisted. "There was this weird brown door open upstairs. I could smell the cake—so I turned into a bloodhound and came down here sniffing for it. When I found this cake just sitting there, I took a piece. Then I got lost trying to get back. That's when I began following the flower petals."

"Mine," Poison Ivy said modestly.

"Beast Boy, show us where you found the cake," Batgirl said. "And hurry. Katana's life may depend on it."

"I can try to remember," Beast Boy said. "But it's like a maze down here!"

As they made their way down the ever-darkening and narrowing passageways, Miss Martian suddenly touched her hand to her temple. Her eyes popped open wide and she pointed into the darkness. "I'm sensing someone's thoughts," Miss Martian said. Her voice was strong. "Oh no! It's Katana, she's . . ."

CHAPTER 3

Two Hours Earlier . . .

"That looks amazing!" Katana said to Steve Trevor. He was proudly holding up a gorgeous, towering purple-and-black cake. "I especially like the yellow Batgirl logo on the top."

"Thank you," Steve said, beaming. "It's spun sugar. I'm not going to tell you how many I had to make before I got one that was perfect! Um, will Wonder Woman be at the party?"

Katana had volunteered to pick up the cake for Batgirl's Hero of the Month party. Steve had a crush on one of her best friends, Wonder Woman, and Katana often teased the two of them. Even though Steve was not a super hero, Wonder Woman had been convinced he was, because whenever they smiled at each other, she felt weak in the knees.

Steve was one of the good guys, unlike some of the Carmine Anderson Day School boys who sat in the middle of the café, flinging food and lasers and icicles at each other—and anyone who even looked in their direction. There was a reason the school's name had been shortened to CAD (Criminals and Delinquents) Academy.

"I'll make sure Wonder Woman knows you made this!" Katana assured him. She ducked when Captain Cold tried to freeze her. Then when he lobbed an icicle at her, Katana held the cake up high above her head with one hand, and with the other hand used her sword to deflect the ice, slicing it into cubes that fell neatly into a nearby table's glasses of strawberry lemonade.

"You've got to do better than that if you want to catch me off guard," Katana chided Captain Cold. She picked up a coaster and threw it like a ninja star. It sliced through the air before knocking his hamburger out of his hand and into his lap.

He glared at Katana while his friends doubled over with laughter.

She smiled. It was fun putting bullies in their place.

Not wanting to be late, Katana headed straight back to school. Wonder Woman and Bumblebee were in charge of the other snacks and decorations. Poison Ivy was handling the flowers, of course. But the cake was to be the centerpiece of the celebration! Katana couldn't wait. Ever since she was a little girl, she had loved parties. She remembered how her grandmother could turn even a boring meal for two into a fabulous party by telling stories, and singing, and smiling so bright that she lit up the room.

On the way back to Super Hero High, Katana was practically dancing, doing kicks and fighting imaginary enemies to protect the cake. Steve had outdone himself! The cake was gorgeous. Batgirl was going to be so surprised!

As she neared Super Hero High's iconic Amethyst Tower, Katana felt a strange sensation wash over her. Was it her lunch, she wondered? Sometimes the ambrosia salad did that to her, especially if it was heavy on the maraschino cherries. Katana loved maraschino cherries.

No, no. It was something else. An unsettling feeling nested in the pit of her stomach. As she headed inside toward the Bat-Bunker to join the party, Katana passed a small doorway near the dining hall. Why had she never noticed it before? The small sturdy door looked out of place in the new and shiny halls of Super Hero High. A sign in Parasite's messy handwriting warned, *Keep out.* And as if an afterthought were the words *Or else,* followed by *That means you. I am serious.*

Curious, Katana tried the rusted doorknob. It wasn't

locked! The door swung open easily. Knowing she needed to get the cake to the party, Katana reminded herself to come back later to check it out. But then something or someone silently beckoned.

"Katana . . ." She thought she heard her name in whispers. "Katana . . ."

What was it?

What was happening?

Katana became distracted, forgetting that everyone was waiting for her. Still carrying the cake, she ventured through the doorway. A salty cool breeze blew back her long black hair as she squinted, trying to adjust her eyes to the darkness. Along the corridor barely lit lightbulbs flickered, throwing off smidgens of light and shadow. Though the passageways weaved, sometimes in circles, Katana set out as if she knew where she was headed—as if she was being drawn to whereabouts unknown.

At last, with her heart racing, Katana faced a heavy metal door covered in rust and barnacles. It was bolted shut with a dozen locks. The salty scent in the air was even thicker. Katana set the cake down. It was still in pristine condition.

The locks were puzzles unto themselves. Katana removed a red-lacquered hairstick from her hair. Then she set to work. With practiced precision, she inserted the stick into each lock, twisting, listening, releasing, opening. She had always been good at mazes and puzzles. At last, the final lock popped open. By now, Katana's hands were starting to tremble. Her heart was racing. She wasn't even sure what she was doing under the school, but something kept propelling her forward.

Katana took a deep breath to calm herself, then pushed hard against the heavy door. It swung as if welcoming her. She stepped inside, her sword drawn and the cake left behind. The wide corridor was dark, with only a pin of light in the distance. Katana walked along a narrow ledge before jumping down into a passageway that looked like an endless tunnel. A cool breeze washed over her. She stood still, welcoming the calm. But it wasn't to remain that way for long.

Katana heard it first before she could see it. A giant *whoosh*ing sound, growing louder with each heartbeat. Even though Captain Cold was nowhere near, Katana stood frozen, not believing what was headed straight at her.

A tall wall of black water was barreling down the tunnel. Laden with silver shards, it glistened, blinding Katana yet mesmerizing her at the same time. As the water threatened to engulf her, Katana tried to call out for help—but even if she could have screamed, who would hear her so deep in the tunnels under Super Hero High?

CHAPTER 4

The water threatened to hit Katana hard. She had seen waves like this only once before, when a tsunami had almost devastated her small seaside village. There was no time to escape. Katana braced herself. From her training she knew how to stand strong, yet bend with the forces coming at her. She gasped as the cold water almost knocked her over, then spun into a vortex of black and silver. At once afraid and intrigued as the water continued to circle, Katana watched in horror as it rose higher, up to her waist, glistening with what looked like sharp silver blades.

Yet it was as if Katana had a seal of protection around her. The waves were starting to settle; the blades did not touch her. Instead, they surrounded her but stayed inches away. So focused was she that Katana did not hear the cries.

"*Look!* It's the cake!"

"She must be nearby!"

"Katana? Katana, where are you, we're coming!"

"Katana!" Batgirl called out from the ledge that ran alongside the tunnel of water. "Are you okay?"

Katana looked up, surprised to find her friends gaping at her with shock on their faces.

"Don't come any closer!" Katana warned. "Blades," she added by way of explanation.

Everyone stared as the water slowed to a stop. Katana could feel her heart racing as the blades twirled with graceful danger around her.

"Could they be . . . ? They look like . . . But that doesn't make any sense. . . ." Gingerly, she reached for one and pulled it out of the water. As she held the blade aloft, the others glanced at one another, unsure what to make of it.

"They're swords!" Poison Ivy exclaimed. "Katana, you are surrounded by swords."

These were not just any swords. No, the swords that circled Katana were elaborate, with handles carved from teak and gold. Precious stones and metals adorned some of them, and each one was different—a masterpiece unto itself.

Still wary of making any fast moves, Katana looked up at a green seagull flying above. It was Beast Boy. "Look there," he said, motioning to a sword that had floated peacefully to the surface of the water. A conch shell was balanced perfectly on the sword's blade.

Katana leaned over and picked up the shell, studying it. Something about it was familiar. When she was younger, she used to walk the beach near Tottori, the coastal prefecture where her family resided. She loved collecting seashells—scallops, a nautilus or two, and sometimes starfish.

In the palm of her hand, the shining conch shell reminded Katana of the top of a swirly soft-serve ice cream cone. There were layers of delicate pink and brown on the outside and a rim of bumps around it. Inside, it seemed to glow an orange-red. Though smaller than the ones she had collected as a girl, this one was still beautiful and majestic. Katana's own conch shell collection sat on her dresser back home. Her grandmother used to say, "These shells were once homes for ocean snails. But when the snails move on, the conch shells remain, collecting stories, memories, and treasures. However, one must listen carefully to the conch shell to learn its secrets."

"Listen carefully," Miss Martian said.

"What?" Katana asked. She hadn't even noticed Miss Martian hiding behind Supergirl.

"Listen to the shell," Miss Martian continued. Her eyes were closed. "It wants to tell you something."

Poison Ivy and Supergirl glanced at each other. Miss Martian seemed to be on the same wavelength as Katana.

Katana raised the shell to her ear. She heard nothing—not

even the quiet, hollow hum one would normally hear in a shell. As she was about to set it down, Miss Martian urged her, "Listen to the shell!"

Embarrassed by her outburst, Miss Martian slowly began to fade until she had disappeared completely.

Seagull Beast Boy landed on Supergirl's shoulder. "Well, that was weird," he noted. He pulled on her hair with his beak.

"Shoo!" Supergirl said, brushing him off.

Batgirl said to Katana, "I think you should try to listen to the shell again."

Katana nodded and lifted it to her ear once again. Everyone was silent. Even Beast Boy.

Katana's eyes widened. The shell began to whisper in her ear.

"It makes no sense," Katana said, listening closely. "It's some sort of riddle, I think."

"What did you hear?" Supergirl asked.

"It said:

> These Samurai swords
> Entrusted to Katana
> The story unfolds."

"Who was talking?" Beast Boy asked.

"Was it a male or female voice?" Batgirl added.

"I really couldn't tell." Katana shook her head. "It was soft and I had to listen closely to catch it. This may sound weird, but it's as if the ocean were speaking to me."

"That's crazy!" Beast Boy said. "And totally cool. I want to talk to the ocean!"

"You can talk to the ocean anytime," Supergirl pointed out. "But getting it to talk back to you is more difficult."

Poison Ivy remarked, "The shell said 'the story unfolds.' What story would that be?"

"Why are the swords entrusted to me?" Katana wondered out loud. Still in the water, she slowly waded toward the others, careful to avoid the swords. "Batgirl, what do you think?"

Batgirl leaned down from the dry ledge and took the shell from Katana. "This really is a mystery," she said, taking photos and then X-raying the shell using the micro-tools from her Utility Belt.

"Careful, don't break them!" Katana called out to Supergirl. She was flying above the water, fishing the swords out and handing them to Poison Ivy to stack alongside the ledge so Batgirl could catalog each one.

"We can't just leave them in the water," Batgirl said.

Katana added, "I don't know what kind of shape they're in. They look like antiques."

Beast Boy carried in what was left of Batgirl's cake and sat cross-legged on the ledge in the form of a bear cub. "There must be three thousand swords here!"

"One hundred," Batgirl corrected him as the last one was pulled out of the water. "There are one hundred swords."

"I have to protect them," Katana said to no one in particular.

"From what?" Beast Boy asked, licking cake from his green paw.

"The conch shell is trying to tell me something," Katana continued.

> These Samurai swords
> Entrusted to Katana
> The story unfolds.

"It's a haiku," she explained.

"A high-who?" Beast Boy asked through a mouthful of cake. "Hey, Batgirl, want some of your cake? It's delish!"

"Haiku! Of course," Batgirl chimed in. "A haiku," she explained to Beast Boy, "is a three-line poem with seventeen syllables."

Katana was studying the swords. "We need to find a clean, dry place to store these," she said. "I have no idea how long they've been in the water, and the moisture in this tunnel might rust them."

"Katana's right," Batgirl said. "We should put the swords

someplace safe. Supergirl, check out this map. There should be a sealed room two levels up and to the southwest." Before she could finish asking "Can you go check it out?" Supergirl had gone and come back.

"It's perfect," Supergirl reported. "I've unsealed the room and cleaned it up. Now all we have to do is move the swords."

It didn't take long to get the swords safely in place. Katana gave them one last look before Batgirl secured a lock on the door, "Just in case," she said. "We'll keep them secure until we figure out why they're here and who they belong to."

Thanks to Poison Ivy's trail of petals, the Supers headed out of the darkened corridors and back to the dorms.

"Katana!" Hawkgirl and The Flash cried out when the group finally entered the Bat-Bunker. "You're safe!"

Katana offered her a subtle smile. "I'm safe!" she said, hoping that was the truth. The caverns, the wall of water, the swords . . . what did they mean?

"Hey! Where have you all been?" Harley asked, looking miffed.

"Cake, anyone?" Beast Boy offered up what was left. He patted his belly. "Oh man, why did you let me eat so much?" he said to Supergirl.

"I didn't—" Supergirl started to say.

"So where have you been?" Harley demanded. She turned on her video camera. "Everyone was looking for you!"

"You're not going to believe this, but—" Beast Boy began.

"We were playing hide-and-seek!" Katana said, cutting him off.

"Aww," Harley cried. "I'm so good at that—next time invite me!"

"But, we weren't—" Beast Boy started to protest.

Katana pulled him aside. "This is a real mystery. Let's keep it our secret for the moment. Until we know more, it will be easier to keep the swords safe if only we know about it. And besides, we still have a Hero of the Month to celebrate!" Katana said, smiling at Batgirl.

CHAPTER 5

That night, Katana panicked as an ocean of water washed over her. She sat up gasping for breath, then realized that she had woken up in a cold sweat. Katana tried to calm herself as she had learned to do when she was young. It had been ages since she had had this nightmare.

In it, her grandmother, Onna-bugeisha Yamashiro, had disappeared. As much as Katana begged and pleaded, no one would tell her what had happened to her grandmother. Not her mother. Not her father. No one would say a word. So Katana set out to find out on her own. As she searched the mountains and the deserts and the oceans of her dream, Katana sensed that someone—or something—was chasing her, getting closer and closer, and just as it was about to grab her, she'd wake up screaming.

"Are you okay?" a worried voice asked.

Katana was surprised to find Bumblebee flying over her

in her pajamas. "I'm fine," Katana said, embarrassed. "Just a bad dream." She yawned and stretched her arms. "Sorry to wake you. Oh wow, I'm tired. I'd better get back to sleep."

"Okay," Bumblebee said, rubbing her eyes. "Just wanted to make sure everything was all right."

"Everything's great," Katana said, stretching her arms over her head again. "Oh, I'm so sleepy! Good night."

When she was sure Bumblebee was gone, Katana opened her eyes and stared into the darkness. Quiet filled the room. Though her grandmother had been gone for several years, Katana missed her now more than ever. Onna would have been able to talk to her about the mysterious haiku.

Liberty Belle looked splendid in her new hat. It was a scale replica of the Liberty Bell from Independence Hall, although fellow teacher Crazy Quilt had insisted on mending the crack in it. Katana, whom many considered a cutting-edge dresser, had always admired her history teacher's style.

On the walls were posters of the larger-than-life super hero battles, like *War of the Gods* and *Reign of the Supermen*, and holographic photos of famous super heroes from history, including some teachers who currently taught at Super Hero High, like Doc Magnus, who understood more about robotics than anyone in the known solar system.

Beast Boy nudged Bumblebee, who was sitting in front of him. "What?" she whispered.

"Buzz buzz," Beast Boy said.

"Buzz buzz, what?" Bumblebee asked, confused.

"Buzz off!" he said, laughing at his own joke.

"That's not funny," Big Barda whispered loudly, poking him with her Mega Rod.

"It was just a joke," Beast Boy said, looking sullen for a moment, before his usual happy-go-lucky demeanor quickly returned.

"Supers!" the teacher called out, ringing the miniature Liberty Bell that sat on her desk. "I want your attention. I've got some great news for you."

Hawkgirl sat up straight and folded her hands on the desk. Batgirl got out a computer pad to take notes. Cyborg set his memory circuit to record.

"We will be embarking on an exciting new assignment," Liberty Belle began. "It's called 'Know Your Place in Your World: A Legacy Project'! We will study your past and relate it to the present while forecasting the future. I know, right? Super exciting!"

Not all the students shared Liberty Belle's enthusiasm. Some Supers had been raised in households where their parents and grandparents were constantly talking about who they were and where they came from. Others did not have a super hero pedigree but longed to create one of their own. And still others saw this as just another boring homework assignment.

"For example," Liberty Belle said, looking around the room. "Bumblebee, you will explore your roots in Metropolis. Beast Boy, Africa, and Wonder Woman, Paradise Island. Miss Martian—*Miss Martian,* are you here?" She looked at the apparently empty chair and smiled at it warmly. "Miss Martian, you will write about Mars, and, Katana, you will explore your ancestry in Japan and your place in the world."

Katana nodded. Just what *was* her place in the world? she wondered.

"This is going to be great!" Batgirl said. Her eyes shone bright as she adjusted the cowl Katana had made for her in Crazy Quilt's costume design class.

"I dunno," Big Barda said, looking glum. "This is all about families, and what about those of us who don't have any?"

Supergirl, who was sitting across the room, had zoomed in on the conversation using her super-hearing. A note plopped down onto Big Barda's desk. *Let's talk later,* it read.

The two looked at each other in agreement.

In the dining hall that night there was the usual chaos. Arrowette shot an arrow through Cyborg's tuna fish sandwich just as he was about to take a bite, and sent it flying. El Diablo heated up his undercooked chicken casserole with a fiery blast from his hand, and Frost cooled it down for him with a breath of cold air. Cheetah accidentally-on-purpose spilled her green Jell-O in front of Lady Shiva. Everyone laughed as Lady Shiva slipped on it. But Lady Shiva had the last laugh as she made a graceful acrobatic landing without spilling a single item on her tray. She bowed to the applause from the students at the surrounding tables.

Parasite, the janitor, just grumbled at another mess to clean up. He hated cleaning up the students' messes and wasn't shy about letting them know it. But since he was on parole, he had no choice.

"He's forbidden to use his powers—the ability to drain others of theirs," Bumblebee told Katana as she poured a pitcher of honey over her spaghetti while Batgirl tried not to make a face. Hawkgirl was talking so animatedly about Venezuela that Harley grinned enthusiastically and exclaimed, "I'm seeing a Harley's Quinntessentials Web special here!"

Big Barda and Supergirl had their heads together, but Katana could hear them.

"I hate stuff like this," Barda said. She pushed her mashed

potatoes around on her plate and buried her vegetables.

At first Katana thought Barda was talking about her meal. That was, until Supergirl put her hand on Barda's shoulder and said, "I know. I'm an orphan, too. But don't you want to know more about where you came from and what the history of your planet was like? I want to remember everything I can about Krypton. Now that it's gone, it's up to me to honor the memory of my home and that of my friends and family."

"You've got a reason to, but I don't know if I want to write about my past," Barda insisted. "Um, *hello*. My home world is called Apokolips. Its entire culture is based on warmongering. I was raised to subjugate any planet I came across. Not exactly school-paper material, do you think?"

Supergirl offered her a smile. "I don't know. That sounds very, um, exciting. We've all got to come from somewhere! Ooh, and your angle can be how you intend to be better than where you came from!"

A slow grin appeared on Barda's face before she good-naturedly swatted Supergirl away with her Mega Rod. The two girls laughed.

Katana pushed her chair back and looked out the window as her friends continued to talk. She smiled because the cherry blossoms were in bloom, even though it was not the season for them. *Thank you, Poison Ivy.*

The blooms made Katana think of her grandmother. She

had been thinking about her a lot lately. What she knew of Onna was that she was strong and kind and loving. Her parents seldom spoke of her after she disappeared, and Katana didn't even know how she died. Maybe this would be a great opportunity to interview them to find out more. Her mom and dad were both professors back in Japan. Surely they would open up to her if Katana said it was a class assignment, right?

CHAPTER 6

The next day there was a meeting of the Junior Detective Society. Everyone was present: Hawkgirl, Batgirl, The Flash, Poison Ivy, Bumblebee, and one special guest—Katana.

Katana looked around Poison Ivy's room. She had often admired how it was colorfully decorated and how there were unusual plants in bloom. Plus, there was always something bubbling in glass beakers as part of whatever science experiment Ivy was working on.

Batgirl cleared her throat. "Let the special meeting of the Junior Detective Society come to order. Junior Detectives, please introduce yourselves as we welcome our guest, Katana."

Katana tried not to laugh as her friends introduced themselves. She wanted to blurt out "I know who all of you are!" but understood that they had their protocol. Her grandmother had taught her about that. Samurai had processes and procedures that were strictly adhered to.

"Hawkgirl," Batgirl said once the introductions were done, "will you please tell our guest what we have discovered?"

Hawkgirl stood up, making sure to keep her powerful wings pulled in tight. She cleared her throat and took a small piece of paper out of her pocket. "Katana," Hawkgirl began. "You asked us to help decipher the mysterious haiku from the conch shell."

Katana nodded. *What have they discovered?* she wondered.

> *These Samurai swords*
> *Entrusted to Katana*
> *The story unfolds.*

"Batgirl has run the haiku through several decoder programs, and we have also spent numerous hours discussing its meaning. We believe we know where the swords came from, and in our sleuthing found the answer from someone who is among us."

Katana held her breath. How could someone at the school know where the mysterious swords came from? Who?

Hawkgirl put down her paper and looked at Katana and said, "That someone is Parasite."

Parasite grumbled as he attempted to scrape the green gloppy goo off the high ceiling in the science room. It was particularly sticky this time, and he didn't even want to know what the volatile violet lumps in it were. There were always mishaps (by accident and on purpose) at Super Hero High. But these happened at the science lab on an hourly basis, all under the guise of learning.

Poison Ivy's face flushed as the Junior Detective Society entered the room. She was glad it wasn't her mess this time. A budding scientist, she was known to accidentally blow things up fairly often. Her mishaps were all in the name of science, though. For instance, she was close to developing a powerful truth serum from the pollen of the Lunaria Annua, also known as the Honesty Flower.

"May we have a word with you, Mr. Parasite?" Batgirl asked.

Katana looked around. A couple of windows were broken. The glowing green goop was starting to drip onto the floor. A desk was overturned. Cracked test tubes of bubbling blue liquids spilled on the counters. She was impressed. The room looked cleaner than normal.

The purple-skinned janitor looked down at the group from atop his ladder. "Busy!" he growled, adding under his breath to no one in particular, ". . . always expecting me to clean up their messes!"

"What if we helped you?" Poison Ivy suggested, picking up a mop. "We could talk while we help you clean."

When Katana saw Parasite hesitate, she added, "When we work together, things are more efficient and go faster."

"Yes," The Flash said. "Then you would have time to relax and answer a couple of questions."

"Am I being accused of something?" Parasite asked. His eyes narrowed defiantly.

"Not at all!" Poison Ivy insisted. "Quite the opposite. We've heard that you know a lot about the darker side of super hero history and lore—*and* no one knows the grounds of Super Hero High like you do."

Parasite puffed up a bit. "Well, I'm glad you think so. None of the teachers would ever think of asking me anything other than to clean up their classrooms. Okay, then," he said, tossing some rags to Hawkgirl, who immediately began to carefully scrub the massive computer board that took up the back wall.

Nimble Katana carefully cleaned the corners and hard-to-reach places, while Poison Ivy used her plants to exude a neutralizing counteragent to the chemical goo oozing all over the lab. And The Flash raced around so quickly that he was nothing but a red blur, but with each lap the room looked cleaner. Soon, the science lab was spotless and ready for a new day of destruction and debris.

"So . . . may we ask you some questions?" Batgirl asked again, referring to her notes on her small wrist computer.

Parasite looked around. The Supers had done a great job. Even he had to admit that. "A deal is a deal," he said. "But I have things to do . . . and I'm awfully tired . . . not enough to eat. G'head, make it fast . . . hit me with what you got."

"Hit you?" Hawkgirl said, defensively making a fist.

"Naw, I mean, ask your questions," Parasite said, rolling his eyes. He relaxed against the teacher's desk at the front of the room, but kept his hand on his mop just in case he needed to make an excuse to get back to work and escape the teens and their questions.

The Supers sat in the front row and Batgirl began as Katana listened in.

"We know there are secret tunnels under the school, and we have reason to believe that they go far beyond Super Hero High," Batgirl said.

Parasite gave an almost imperceptible nod.

"We've seen the sign you wrote on the door near the cafeteria," The Flash said. "So you must be familiar with the underground caverns and passageways."

"We've been there. We know they exist," Hawkgirl said.

"What we don't know is exactly why."

Poison Ivy had been holding a Lunaria Annua. She handed it to Parasite, who awkwardly took it. Ivy smiled warmly at him. "You know so much," she said sincerely. "Our friend Katana has a mystery to solve and could use your help. Will you help us, please, Mr. Parasite, sir?"

Parasite sniffed the flower and tamped down a smile. He nodded slowly.

Katana made a mental note to take a lesson from Poison Ivy. Parasite had spent years as a janitor at the school cultivating his image as a curmudgeonly ex-criminal . . . but now Katana wondered if his grumpiness might be tied to the fact that he was weak and exhausted. Parasite had to refrain from fully using his powers to drain the students and faculty of their energy, and that was hard for him. However, Katana could clearly see that Parasite, like most others, responded to kindness.

"Super Hero High wasn't always new and shiny," he began. "And not fully funded like it is now. In decades past, the school was a series of odd buildings, some of them centuries old. Then suddenly, there was an influx of money—not sure where it came from. Some say it was a private donor whose family had been saved by super heroes—or maybe even a wealthy family *of* super heroes. No one really knows for sure—or maybe someone does. . . ." Parasite chuckled as a smile crossed his mottled face.

Batgirl glanced at her friends. She telegraphed them a look that said she had heard these rumors.

Parasite took the teacher's seat and, getting comfortable, put his hands behind his head. "But there was a new initiative to build this big bright school that we all know today."

Katana wondered how this related to the haiku and the swords. Was this just the beginning?

> These Samurai swords
> Entrusted to Katana
> The story unfolds.

"Most of the old school was just mowed down to make room for the new one. But the underground mazes and rooms remained. The Super Hero High Historical Society didn't want them touched; plus, by then they had expanded past their original uses. Over the years, more and more tunnels and secret rooms were built. Students created unofficial lairs as secret clubhouses, and more and more complex vaults had to be built to store villains' confiscated super weapons. There was a need for this each time the school got destroyed by some evil being—which happened a lot more back in the old days. It's so complex down there, no one knows the full extent of the tunnels and caverns."

"Water?" Batgirl said, seemingly out of nowhere. "Where does the water come from?"

Parasite sat up and folded his hands on the desk like a teacher. "Water," he echoed. "Ah, the old waterways. Yes, yes, that underground water system was used for various things before it was blocked off. At one time it was a transportation system to deliver supplies shipped in sealed pods from other countries. Later, some Supers who had swimming skills or water vehicles used it to access the ocean. But it's been decades since the aqueducts were used." His eyes narrowed. "Why do you want to know?"

"No reason," Katana said. "Well, we were just wondering. If someone wanted to send something to someone but keep it a secret, they could use the—what did you call them? Aqueducts? They could use the aqueducts, right?"

"Water! Oceans! Who needs that wet mess?" Parasite grumbled, returning to his usual demeanor. "But yes, they could do that. The question is, why would anyone *want* to?"

CHAPTER 7

"So how did you even know to go underground to find the swords?" Bumblebee asked. She smiled sweetly, then tried to knock Katana over by blasting her with one of her powerful electric beestings.

Katana sliced the energy blast in half with her sword, but the residual jolt threw her several feet backward, slamming her into a wall with a hard thud. Her lightweight armor, based on a traditional Samurai design but fortified with the strongest modern materials, took the brunt of the impact. Katana dropped gracefully to the ground, ready for more.

The two did this over and over again. Katana and Bumblebee were in phys ed at the moment, where students were teamed up to practice their powers and skills, albeit not at full strength.

"More hitting! More throwing! Less talking!" Wildcat, the school's coach, roared. "This isn't a tea party here! We are learning to defend and fight! Lives could depend on it! Maybe even yours!"

Katana ran at Bumblebee with her sword in hand, lunging at her friend. Bumblebee shrank small and dodged the sharp blade. Both laughed. Intense practice like this was always fun!

"So, I can't explain why I went underground, but I couldn't stop myself," Katana said as she did a martial arts tumble maneuver, landing in a fighting stance. In one hand she held her favorite shuriken, a sharpened four-point throwing star, and in the other were the titanium nunchakus her parents had given her for her birthday. "It was like someone or something was speaking to me, drawing me in. I was sort of like in a trance. All I could think of was that I had to find out who—or *what*—was calling me."

"It happens to me all the time," someone said.

Katana looked around but didn't see anyone. "Miss Martian?" she said aloud.

Slowly, the figure of a green teen appeared before them.

"Hi!" Bumblebee said. The thick golden streak in her dark honey-brown hair glistened in the sun. "Want to be on our team?"

"Really?" Miss Martian said. She looked at her shoes. "But I feel out of place here . . . and in most places, for that matter. Reading minds isn't exactly a phys ed kind of power."

"What you do is incredible," Katana insisted. "Like how you led Batgirl and the other Supers to find me. If not for you, I'd probably still be standing in that aqueduct surrounded by swords, and I'd be all wrinkly from being in the water for so long!"

Miss Martian laughed.

"I asked Katana about why she was drawn to the swords," Bumblebee said. "But she's not sure. Do you have any idea?"

Miss Martian nodded. She watched as Cheetah raced up the side of a building with Supergirl in hot pursuit. "There are times," Miss Martian said, "when we are not in total control of our surroundings, and we let our senses and our thoughts access everything around us. It's like when you are falling asleep. You are still thinking, yet at the same time, other thoughts come unbidden from the corners of your mind, and your other senses start to take over."

Katana nodded, remembering the dream that still plagued her.

"From the impressions I got when trying to find you," Miss Martian continued, "I felt that the conch shell was a message someone or something was sending you. It was very specific."

"What do you mean?" Bumblebee asked. She wrinkled her nose.

"It was a message meant just for Katana," Miss Martian

ventured. "Did anyone else listen to the conch shell?"

"The entire Junior Detective Society," Katana told her.

"And did they hear anything?" asked Miss Martian.

Katana slowly shook her head. "No," she said. "Just me."

Miss Martian looked at Katana and shut her eyes. "You know more than you know," she finally said, before disappearing.

"She talks in riddles," Katana said to Batgirl. Katana was swinging her sword overhead so fast that Batgirl thought it might lift her off the ground like a helicopter. Though school was out for the day, the girls had decided to continue working on their powers and skills since they were having such a great time.

"That's because Miss Martian is scanning brains and getting impressions," Batgirl said as she tested her new grappling tools. Katana admired how she was swinging from trees and looked like she was flying. Batgirl was always trying to create new B.A.T. devices. After that last run-in with Croc, she had started developing a new tear gas that worked specifically on reptile people.

"She doesn't talk to me," Big Barda said. She was swinging her Mega Rod in the air to limber up when a wayward baseball headed toward her from the athletic field. Barda hit the ball and watched as it sailed through the sky toward downtown Metropolis. "I think I scare her," she continued, "but I don't know why."

"Well, Katana," Batgirl said. "What is it that *you* know? I mean, we're all doing our Legacy projects. Have you learned anything that might explain the swords? The conch shell? The haiku?"

Barda sat down on the ground. "I'm in the mood for a good story," she said, making herself comfortable. Batgirl joined her. "Tell us one!"

"Okay, well, here's what I know so far," Katana began.

CHAPTER 8

"I am the granddaughter of the first female Samurai super hero, Onna-bugeisha Yamashiro. My grandmother on my mother's side descended from a long line of Samurai. To honor that side of my family, my mother kept her maiden name and passed it on to me. My grandmother was an only child, as was my mother, as am I.

"Only men were allowed to be official Samurai warriors—they were military nobility and often referred to as Bushi, which means 'those who serve in close attendance to the nobility.' For centuries they were considered heroes. It was uncommon, but some Samurai passed along the skills, philosophies, and code of the Bushido to their daughters. My Onna's family did this, and the women trained alongside the men with the swords. They eventually became known for being as good as, or better than, many of the male Samurai.

"Some even went into battle disguised as men. Wars were

won because of these brave women, though no one ever knew. So strict was the code that only males could battle in the traditional armor.

"By the time my grandmother was born, the Samurai no longer existed. In the 1870s, Emperor Meiji abolished the Samurai, instead favoring a Western-style army. So after hundreds of years, and legacies passed down through generations, the Samurai ceased to exist. At least, that was what people thought."

"*Watch out!*" Beast Boy yelled as he flew over them flapping his seagull wings. He was chasing Supergirl, who was speeding past in an effort to catch up to Wonder Woman, who had just tied up a couple of criminals in her Lasso of Truth in Centennial Park.

"Please keep going," Barda implored. "How can your grandmother be a Samurai super hero if they were disbanded?"

Katana shook her head. "I'm not sure," she said. "Everyone in my family knew about Onna, but no one spoke of it. My mom has always said that I'm not ready to know the whole story yet.

"Growing up, I just knew that Onna would often disappear for days, sometimes weeks, at a time. When she returned, there would be something in the news about a village being saved or a disaster being averted. But it was always a mystery how it was done. Yet there were rumors that a Samurai was somehow responsible.

"Late at night, I'd hear my parents whispering about Onna and how they wished she'd retire. That it was not right for her to keep putting herself in danger. I saw a news program once—it was following up on the legend of the modern Samurai, and when it said that there was one who was considered a super hero Samurai, my mother turned off the television.

"'Don't watch this nonsense,' she said by way of explanation. 'Get back to your studies, Katana.'

"My parents are teachers, so my doing well in school is important to them. Even though I loved books, it was the stories that Onna told me at night that made my heart swell and my imagination soar. She told me tales of good versus evil, and of amazing feats with the sword. I learned about the honor of the Samurai and that service to others was important.

"Onna taught me how to use a sword." Katana got up and began to pace as she spoke. "Even though my parents would have preferred that I have my nose buried in books. But since I got good grades, what could they say? Still, on the news they kept talking about this legendary Samurai super hero, and then there were confirmations that it wasn't just any Samurai, but a female one. Onna and I would try to guess who she was, what her story was about, and where she lived."

Katana stopped and looked off in the distance. Lady Shiva was showing Adam Strange how to do a flying side kick, but he kept slipping and ending up facedown on the ground.

"Please go on," Barda nudged.

"Yeah, we want to know more," Batgirl said.

Katana nodded and continued. "One day, I was walking home from school with a couple of friends. I must have been in third or fourth grade. As we made our way along a narrow, winding road, we passed a house on fire. Inside, a woman was screaming that she was trapped with her children. We froze, not knowing what to do, when suddenly a Samurai in full battle garb appeared out of nowhere. Though her face was covered, we could tell it was a female warrior. She leapt up to the second-floor ledge and brought the mother and her children to safety, then put out the flames using the barrels of rainwater that had been collecting in the garden.

"Before anyone could thank the super hero Samurai, she was gone.

"I raced home, excited to tell Onna what I had just seen. But the house was quiet. 'Onna! Onna!' I yelled out. 'Where are you?'

"'I'm here,' she said. I went quickly to her room. Her hair was wet, and she was drying it with a towel. It was an odd time to take a bath. 'What news do you have?'

"As I began to tell her what I had seen, I could smell something in her room. I looked in the corner, where there were some leaves and cinders. In that moment I knew who the legendary super hero Samurai was."

CHAPTER 9

"*I know, I know!*" Big Barda yelled excitedly, raising her hand. "It was her, your grandmother! Am I right? I know I'm right!"

"Onna knew that I knew. She hugged me tight and told me it was our secret.

"'Momma says it's not good to keep secrets,' I told her.

"She sighed and said, 'Oh, your momma. Yes, it is good to tell the truth, but some things should not be talked about until the time is right. You know my secret, but if you were to tell, it would be harder for me to do my job—to serve the people.'

"'I want to be like you!' I announced. 'Let me be like you! Please teach me.'

"'I don't know how your parents would feel,' my grandmother said. But I could tell she was thinking about it.

"'Please, Onna,' I begged. 'Please.'

"She finally smiled and said, 'We will go slow. I will teach you some basics.'

"On that day, Onna let me hold a sword for the first time—her sword. This very one," Katana said, unsheathing it for Barda and Batgirl to see. "Whenever we practiced, she would let me use it even though I could barely hold it up in the beginning. My grandmother told me, 'I will train you, but it is yet to be seen who you will grow up to be. That will be up to you.'

"Though at first the sword was way too big for me, I cherished it. Every day, Onna and I would walk along the cliffs overlooking the ocean, where she would train me in martial arts, in swordplay, and in the way of the Bushido. We never told my parents, knowing they would prefer I lead the life of an academic. But I didn't want to learn about the world from books, I wanted to live it, and more than anything I wanted to be like Onna and be worthy enough to one day be called a Samurai super hero."

"I'll bet your grandmother is so proud that you are at Super Hero High," Batgirl said.

Katana bowed her head. "Onna is no longer with us. She never knew that I made it here."

"What happened?" Barda said. Her eyes grew big.

Katana shrugged. "I don't know. No one will tell me. I just know that one day after helping her get into her Samurai armor, she kissed me as she always did before going out. Before she left, she turned around and handed me her sword. 'Keep this safe and it will keep you safe,' she told me. That night she didn't come home." A note of sorrow swelled in Katana's voice. "That was the last time I saw her."

Big Barda's eyes filled with tears. "I'm not crying," she grumbled to Batgirl. "You are!"

Batgirl wiped her eyes with the back of her hand then gave Katana a hug. Barda hung back for a second and watched, then finally said, "Oh well. Okay, why not?" and joined the group hug.

"Thank you," Katana said, savoring the embrace of her friends. "This means a lot to me."

"Got it!" someone yelled. It was Harley. "Love this!" She turned her camera on herself. "Here at Super Hero High, camaraderie runs rampant. Just a few short months ago, Big Barda was the enemy, and now here she is, being accepted and embraced by the indomitable Katana and our recent Hero of the Month, Batgirl."

Katana broke from the hug. "Put the camera down, Harley," she said. "This is private."

Harley pouted. "Ah, man. You guys are no fun!" she said. "Everyone loves to see personal *private* moments on video! It's like peeking, but even more fun!"

"Look!" Batgirl said, distracting her. "Isn't that Hawkgirl

flying alongside that plane with engine trouble?"

As Harley raced off in the hopes of getting an exclusive, Katana turned to Batgirl and Barda. "Thank you for listening to me. Sharing my story with you brings me closer to my Onna." Katana paused, then added wistfully, "Oh, what I would give to see her just once more."

CHAPTER 10

"Katana, please step forward," Crazy Quilt announced. He was dressed in his usual array of brightly colored clothes. On anyone else the outfit would have looked like a collision of paint swatches. However, Crazy Quilt made it look like a fashion statement extraordinaire.

Katana rose from the back of the room, stepping over Cheetah's outstretched legs. While some students, like Supergirl, were a little klutzy, and others, like Big Barda, tended to stomp, Katana had the posture and grace of a ballerina. In Wildcat's phys ed class, she was able to run the five-mile course with a dozen books balanced on her head and a bowl of goldfish on top of the books, without losing one drop of water or a single fish.

"Up, up!" Crazy Quilt said as a marble pedestal rose from the floor. "Now, Katana, strike a pose!"

Katana stood tall with her arms at her sides. "No! No!"

her teacher called out. "Be dramatic! Make a statement! Wow us! Like this . . ."

Quilty, as he was sometimes called behind his back, lunged forward with his hands on his hips and his head thrown back. He looked just as chic as he had in his youth when he had graced the cover of the *Super Hero Supermodels* magazine he kept displayed on his desk—with a tiny spotlight shining on it.

Katana suddenly thought about the swords. It was strange, but ever since they had been put safely away, it was like they had become a hazy idea to her, coming in and out of her thoughts like the ebb and flow of the tide—real, but not real.

"And pose!" Crazy Quilt shouted. "Katana. Earth to Katana—strike a pose!"

Katana hated drawing attention to herself. She knew Crazy Quilt wouldn't give up, however—he loved a grand fashion pose. So she mimicked what he had done, even though it felt awkward and must've looked even more so. How could Star Sapphire, who sometimes modeled for fashion magazines, stand it? Katana wondered.

Crazy Quilt beamed as he circled her. "Now, future fashion mavens, I want you all to look at Katana's costume. Stylish? Yes! But functional as well. Katana, dear, show the class how your custom-made material stretches in all the right places."

Katana stood en pointe and with a flourish leapt down from the pedestal. She tucked into herself, rolled across the room, then sprang up and backflipped, landing on the pedestal once more.

"See!" her teacher pointed out. He motioned to her black skirt with red ribbon trim. "No wrinkles! And her leggings have give and support at the same time. Plus, look at those sleek lines! And the armor, and those lace-up boots! They are to die for," he said, swooning. "Plus, they're functional, functional, functional! Show them, Katana!"

In a single motion, Katana swept her arm down and retrieved a dagger from her boot. Without stopping, her hand reached around her waist to a metal chain, which she tossed across the room. It cut the air, making a barely audible whipping sound as it wrapped around a mannequin. The chain was followed by a dagger that knocked the faux blaster out of its plastic hand.

Crazy Quilt applauded and cried "Brava! Brava!" as Katana stood in a fighting stance, her sword now drawn. "Brava!"

As Katana made her way back to her seat, Star Sapphire smiled and played with the purple ring on her finger. Star Sapphire looked sincere, and Katana felt a wave of kindness wash over her as she passed.

"That whole Samurai thing is *so* overdone," Sapphire

whispered to Cheetah. The feline nodded and sharpened her nails with a file.

On their way across campus to June Moone's art class, Katana and Poison Ivy passed a large patch of fast-growing, spiky kirbo weeds that threatened to cover up the statue of a famed super hero named Tsunami, who could swim at superhuman speed. The two looked at each other, and without saying anything, Katana cut down the kirbo with her sword, and Ivy created a lovely garden where the weeds had once resided. A small canopy of cherry- and orange-blossom trees circled the space, and an assortment of daisies, roses, and orchids accentuated the oasis. The scent of blossoms and blooms was intoxicating.

"Got it!" Harley announced as she executed a perfect double handspring and then a backflip while somehow still filming. "This will be on Harley's Quinntessentials before you can say 'What's up at Super Hero High?'" Harley hesitated a beat. "Hey, does it have a name?"

Katana bowed to Poison Ivy, giving her the honor.

"Harmony Garden?" Ivy suggested.

"Perfect." Harley beamed as she turned the camera back on herself. "Harmony Garden! You saw it here first, fans!"

In June Moone's art class, Katana stared at the block of wood in front of her. It was a little larger than a shoe box. A regular shoe box, not one for her leather lace-up boots with hidden panels for weapons. Like Onna's, Katana's boots were custom-made by a famous shoemaking family in Kyoto that had been catering to Samurai for generations.

As Katana continued her stare-down with the block of wood, her teacher whirled around, her green silk dress twirling around her.

"Art is about expression!" Ms. Moone declared. "It should enchant and move one's emotions. That is your assignment for today. Turn the different materials in front of you into something that reflects your feelings!"

As the Supers set to work, Katana scanned the room. Hawkgirl was turning a lump of clay into a soaring sculpture of a bird in flight. Supergirl was using glue, string, and sequins to make a rainbow heart. Batgirl was making a digital LED display with the words super*POW*ers, brain*POW*er, and will*POW*er.

The wood remained on Katana's desk untouched. What did she feel inside, she wondered. So much of what she did and thought was controlled. It was not like her to become unhinged, as Harley sometimes did, or overly excited about things, like Bumblebee, or intense, like Big Barda, though she was so much better now than when she had first come to Super Hero High.

No, Katana was measured, and though she was fun to be around, there were questions inside her that were confusing and feelings that weren't addressed. And mysteries, like what had happened to her Onna . . . and why the swords had suddenly appeared.

"How are you doing, Katana?" Ms. Moone asked, looking over her shoulder.

"It's hard for me to get started," Katana admitted. She noticed that no one else in the room seemed to have that problem. The Flash was already done with his art project, a finger-painted blueprint of the entirety of Super Hero High and surrounding streets of Metropolis.

"Not every piece of art has to be a masterpiece," her teacher reminded her star student. "Sometimes it's just a starting place."

Katana was used to her paintings and sculptures being praised and held up to the class as examples of what to strive for. Her oils of a cherry tree in bloom had been in the lobby of the school, and she had won awards for her art.

In the past, when Katana approached an art project, she knew exactly what she wanted to do and see. This time was different. She picked up the block and turned it over and over again. Then she stood and held it up in front of her, tossing it into the air. Before it could land, Katana had whipped out her sword and attacked it, leaping high, whirling around, slicing and dicing.

Wood chips flew around her like snowflakes blown by a wild winter wind.

"Whoa!" Beast Boy said. He was just finishing a fluorescent painting on velvet, of a creature with the snout of a pig, the ears of a bat, the slicked-back fur of a platypus, and the smile of . . . Beast Boy.

When the sawdust settled, June Moone stared and her green eyes widened. *"This,"* she announced triumphantly, "this is what I'm talking about when I say that art elicits emotion and vice versa! Take a bow, Katana."

As Katana did as she was told, she could hear Raven mutter, "Teacher's pet. I can't even tell what that thing is."

Katana wasn't really sure what it was, either. Only that it was how she felt. When class ended, she started to leave her art piece behind. Suddenly, Miss Martian became visible and asked shyly, "May I keep it?"

"Go ahead. It's yours," Katana said. "I don't even know why I made it."

Miss Martian smiled and held the intricate Japanese box puzzle to her chest, hugging it. The outside boasted a hexagonal pattern that moved if one stared at it. When she rattled the box she could hear something inside. "What is it?" Miss Martian asked. "What's inside?"

Katana shook her head, surprised. She had not put anything in it. "I don't know," she answered honestly.

CHAPTER 11

That night, Katana slipped out of her dorm room. It was easier said than done. Supergirl was set on having another one of her cookie parties—her aunt Martha had sent her biweekly box of homemade snickerdoodle, chocolate chip, and peanut butter cookies. Wonder Woman had decided that everyone should organize their rooms—she thought getting organized was a great way to have fun. And the Junior Detective Society wanted to talk to Katana about the haiku.

Katana was slowly getting to know the underground corridors. Yet, even though she carried a lantern, it did little to penetrate the darkness of the seemingly endless labyrinth. Though she had a keen sense of direction, Katana was often lost on her infrequent visits to the swords. It was weird, but the aqueduct that brought the swords had dried up. Not a drop of water was left. She opened the door to where the swords now rested and put down her lantern. Instantly, the room was bathed in a warm glow. The sound of metal startled her as the swords stood upright at attention, like soldiers.

Katana paused, waiting to see if something would happen. When it did not, she picked up the sword closest to her and examined it. It was heavier than the one Onna had given her, and much more ornate, with pearl inlays and a dragon carved into the handle. She tried it out. It felt good in her hands. Then she tried another and another. Each one had its own feel and strength. Each one was unique. Like being in the Harmony Garden that Poison Ivy had recently created, Katana felt a kind of peace and comfort just being in their presence.

The mystery of the swords was as confounding to Katana as her grandmother's disappearance years earlier. Though she had heard her parents whisper of what might have happened, they always stopped talking when she was near. Maybe, Katana thought, it was time to be bold and just ask.

"Hi, Mom!" Katana said, looking straight into the computer. She knew that her parents hated AboutFace, but Katana had some questions and was certain that if she told them it was for a school assignment, they'd answer them. "Is Dad there?"

"I'm here!" a deep voice said off camera.

"You have to sit closer to me," her mother said jokingly. "I won't bite."

"Like this?" he asked. Katana could see her father's shoulder. In that moment she realized how much she missed her parents.

"Hi, Kat!" her father said, leaning so far into the camera that now all she could see was the tip of his nose. She would have thought that after all this time, they would have figured out AboutFace.

"Hey, Dad!" she said.

"How are your grades?" her father asked.

"All As," Katana reported. "Well, one B in science," she said quickly, hoping they wouldn't hear. "But I have an A-plus in art!"

"Let's try for all As, shall we?" her mother said.

"Try?" her dad said. "Let's do it! We can do it, right, Kat?"

Katana sighed. She wished her parents weren't so grade-oriented. But then, that was their world—academia. After all, they were professors. They had even met in college. School was sort of their life.

"So I have a project for my history class," Katana began. "Our teacher said we're supposed to interview our relatives."

"That would be us!" her father quipped. A smile appeared on the screen just under his nose. He was very proud of his jests and would often say, "See! I'm not just a fuddy-duddy old professor, I'm punny!"

"Katana, what would you like to know?" her mother asked. Her eyes were bright, and her small nose and strong jaw reminded Katana of Onna. Her grandmother had often said that she had hoped her daughter would follow in the family business, but that she would support whatever she decided to do. So when Katana shared that she wanted to be a Samurai, Onna was thrilled, even though her parents were not.

"Well, we're doing family legacy projects," Katana explained. She held up her notes as evidence. "Looking back at the history of where we came from. How influences of the past help determine who we are today, and where we might be headed."

Both parents nodded. Katana continued, "I'd like the focus of my project to be Onna." She noted that her mother's smile froze on her face and that her father's jaw tightened. "But I need to know more about her." Katana hesitated. "Like what happened to her."

There was a long, awkward silence. Finally, her father spoke to Katana's mother. "Maybe it's time for our daughter to know the truth," he said.

Katana's heart quickened. After all these years, she would finally find out where Onna had gone, and why she had never said goodbye. Afraid that if she spoke, her parents might change their minds, Katana remained silent.

Her mother blinked nervously and her father put his arm around her. "Dearest," she said to her daughter. "Your father is right. You are old enough, and strong enough, to know the truth." She took several deep breaths, as if trying to gather her courage.

Katana reached for a pad of paper to take notes.

Her mother looked down at her lap and then directly into the camera. "Your grandmother," she said slowly, "was a Samurai super hero." Katana nodded. This much she knew, even if no one had told her.

"Onna was very secretive about her assignments," her mom continued. "On her last one she was meeting a classmate of hers. Like you, when she was a teen she attended a special high school to supplement her years of training as a Samurai warrior. Her classmate was, I later heard, a very willful creature who had long admired Onna.

"Your grandmother was looking forward to reuniting with this old friend of hers. He too had amazing powers and skills, and she relished being in the presence of those like her."

Katana glanced at her bulletin board filled with photos of her friends and knew how her grandmother had felt.

Her mother hesitated before continuing. "Onna never

returned from that meeting. There were rumors that her old classmate had betrayed her. Why he might have done it and what he wanted, we will never know. We only know she perished."

Both Katana and her mom were now in tears. "It is dangerous being a super hero," her mother cautioned. "But if that is your will, if that is what your heart desires, we will not stand in your way. That is what Onna would have wanted."

Katana couldn't breathe. What she had feared all along, what she had known in her heart to be true—that Onna had died—was now a confirmed reality. She wished she were with her mom and dad so they could embrace her, and she them. Both looked like they were in deep pain, just like her.

Katana thanked her parents and bid them goodbye. As she sat alone in her room with the news of her Onna, Katana felt hollow. Looking around for something to comfort her, she reached for the conch shell. When she held it tight, it brought her some comfort. Onna had loved the sea. Then Katana mustered the strength to do something out of character.

"Batgirl," she said, using her com bracelet, "I need you. And bring Barda, too."

In an instant, both were in her room. When they saw how upset she was, neither asked any questions. Instead, they did what friends do. They wrapped Katana in a huge, long hug.

CHAPTER 12

Katana was quiet the next day. If Bumblebee and others noticed, they didn't say anything, and gave her some space. Many of the Supers often retreated into bubbles of silence when the world, or high school, or just being a teen got overwhelming. There was that time when Wonder Woman had thought of returning to her home on Themyscira, or the times when Batgirl had retreated to her Bat-Bunker just because she wanted time alone with her tech.

As Katana headed to Liberty Belle's history class, Harley ran up and skipped alongside her. "Cat got your tongue?" she quipped.

They passed by Cheetah, who gave them a mischievous smile.

"Just a lot to think about," Katana said diplomatically. Unlike Starfire or Beast Boy, who didn't filter or hold back, Katana kept her innermost feelings to herself.

"You can tell me!" Harley said. Her eyes twinkled. She leapt in front of Katana and blocked her way, turning on her camera. "I won't tell anyone." She winked.

When Harley refused to budge, Katana leapt over her. Then Harley leapt over Katana. This went on all the way to class, like an odd version of super hero leapfrog.

"Harley," Katana finally said, crossing her arms. "I need some privacy. Can you understand that?"

Harley grinned and turned the camera off. "Sure, sure, sure," she said. "But I know you have a big story in you somewhere, and when you're ready to tell it, I get first dibs, right?"

Katana smiled. Harley's boundless enthusiasm and energy were hard to resist. "Of course," she said. "You got it!"

As Harley ran away, yelling, "Flash, Flash, slow down, I wanna talk to you! My viewers want to know: *what are you running from?*"

Katana wondered if she'd ever know what her story was.

Though, like her peers, Katana had vowed to fight to make the world a safer place, now more than ever she wanted to live up to her grandmother's legacy. But the confirmation of Onna's death continued to weigh heavily on her, distracting her from the Legacy project and other schoolwork.

"Dr. Arkham will be able to help you," Principal Waller said. "He's starting a weekly meeting called the Family Business, where Supers are encouraged to talk about the pressures and fears of living up to their legacies."

At Waller's request, Katana had come to the principal's office. As someone who was seldom, if ever, in trouble, it was an odd feeling for Katana. Bumblebee, who was Waller's most trusted student assistant, flew in from time to time, delivering notes—though, because she had shrunk herself, it looked like the papers were flying on their own.

Although Amanda Waller was constantly busy running Super Hero High, training the teachers who trained the new Supers, and keeping everything and everyone in line, she had an uncanny ability to be in sync with every student. Sometimes it seemed like Waller knew how her students felt before they did.

"I'm fine," Katana insisted. "Nothing's wrong." She had been raised not to complain or feel sorry for herself.

A full-sized Bumblebee entered and set a tray of tea and honey on the desk. She winked at Katana before she left.

The Wall sat very still, making Katana nervous. Her eyes

were unblinking, and Katana, who was known to be able to stare anyone down, turned away.

"Katana," the principal said. Though her face looked stern, there was kindness in her eyes. "It's okay to feel bad. We all do sometimes. That's what makes us different from robots and drones. I want you to know that I'm here for you. That's a promise I've made to every parent who has entrusted me with their child here at Super Hero High.

"When you first came to us, you told me about your grandmother and how it is your dream to live up to her legacy." Katana nodded. "And now that you've heard her fate, does it make you feel any different about wanting to be here?"

Katana looked up, surprised. "No, no, I still want to be here. I need to be here now more than ever. But wait! You know what happened to my grandmother? How?" *Who told?* she wondered. *Was it Batgirl or Big Barda?*

"Your mother called," the principal said. "She told me. She's worried about you. This is big news to absorb. You shouldn't have to do it alone. I hope you'll join Dr. Arkham's group. You don't have to go if you don't want to, but, Katana, you have a lot of weight on your shoulders right now, and we want to help you."

Katana considered it. Supergirl and Batgirl had raved about how insightful Dr. Arkham was. What could it hurt?

Dr. Arkham's office was dark and there were stacks of books and papers everywhere, some so tall they threatened to fall over. Katana took a seat in the circle and nodded to her fellow students. All looked a tad embarrassed to be there. She recognized most and was as surprised to see them as they were to see her. For kids who were so bent on helping others, the Supers often had trouble asking for help for themselves.

"This is a closed group," Dr. Arkham assured them. His magnificently bald head was offset by a meticulously groomed beard. His glasses made his eyes seem unusually large. "Thank you for coming to the Family Business support group. No one is required to talk. However, we are here to share the pressures we feel from being in a super hero family. It is difficult, I know, to live up to the hype and responsibilities that others put on you. Or," he added after a dramatic pause, "the pressure you put on yourself."

"My mother is a queen," Wonder Woman said. Katana couldn't believe her friend had problems. Wonder Woman was so strong and self-assured. "I am a warrior princess," she continued, looking down at her hands folded on her lap. "One day I might have to become queen and live up to my mother's legacy—and that's scary to me. It makes stopping Giganta or a few Furies seem easy by comparison."

The others nodded. They each understood.

"My father always compares me to how he was at my age. Plus, he was good at math," Ravager said.

Katana took a deep breath when it was her turn. "I am the granddaughter of a super hero," she began. "But my parents would prefer I wasn't one. They haven't said it outright, but I know this to be true. I also know that what my grandmother did, what she achieved, is a shining example of what it means to serve this world. I only hope to achieve a small portion of what she did. I . . . I . . ."

Katana couldn't put it all into words. Not yet.

"Good start. Thank you for sharing." Dr. Arkham nodded to her and then said, "Let's give someone else a chance to share."

Miss Martian raised her hand. Katana hadn't even known she was in the room.

"Yes, you there in the back," Dr. Arkham said, pointing into the shadows.

"I . . . I'm supposed to be a super hero," Miss Martian began. Everyone strained to hear her. "My family can all read minds, but my powers come and go. I'm afraid I'm letting everyone down."

There was a murmur in the room, and everyone nodded.

The young heroes knew this feeling.

"Go on," Dr. Arkham encouraged Miss Martian.

"Sometimes I can read minds clearly," she said. Several Supers looked nervous, and even Dr. Arkham shifted in his seat. "Other times I only get faint impressions. My uncle says I need to be more confident. More assured. And, um . . . that's hard for me. . . ."

Katana watched Miss Martian fade again and made a mental note to be friendlier to her. Katana had seen others dismiss this alien from Mars, but just because she didn't always appear to be in the room didn't mean Miss Martian didn't exist. Plus, not only was she kind, but she had also led Katana's friends to find her and told her about the conch shell. Miss Martian, Katana could tell, was so much more than she appeared to be.

CHAPTER 13

"**W**hat do you mean you're not sure?" Katana heard Harley saying. "It's brilliant! *I'm* brilliant! We will be brilliant!"

They were in the library. Batgirl was shelving books, swinging from the ceiling on her grappling wire to get to the top shelves, and Supergirl was rushing around checking out materials for her Liberty Belle project. Hawkgirl was on the super computer charting her family ancestry, and Beast Boy was polishing off a falafel sandwich. He let out a huge burp, and then grinned when everyone stared at him.

"What?" he asked, clearly proud of himself. "If you think that's big, you should hear what it sounds like after I've had a *really* huge meal in the form of an Apatosaurus."

Katana turned back to see what Harley was up to. She had cornered Miss Martian, who was starting to fade fast. "It's a surefire hit! WHAM!" Harley said, causing Miss Martian to go almost completely invisible. "Everyone will watch it!"

"What's going on?" Katana asked.

The alien forced a weak smile.

"I've got this *wonderful* idea," Harley said, gushing. She did a backflip. "I want to give Miss Martian her own show—a *mind-reading* show. It'll be great for my ratings! She'll be a Harley's Quinntessentials regular. Imagine if she read the minds of those CAD Academy cads, or some celebrities and superstars . . . or best yet: teachers who give pop quizzes. WOWZA!"

Harley turned to where Miss Martian once stood. "Where'd she go? Where'd she go?" she asked, running around the library shouting, "Miss Martian! I want to talk to you."

"Harley's gone," Katana said over her shoulder.

"Thank you," a small voice answered behind her.

"You know, you don't have to do anything you don't want to," Katana assured her.

When she was met with silence, Katana wasn't sure Miss Martian was still there. She almost walked away, when she heard a familiar voice say, "I don't want to use my powers as a gimmick. If I use them at all, I want it to be for good, to help, not for gossip or ratings. It's unethical to read minds except for sharing insights, or for emergencies and life-and-death situations. . . ." As the shy alien spoke, Katana watched her appear before her eyes.

"Don't worry. Harley will have some crazy new idea tomorrow and forget all about the mind-reading segment. But whatever you do, don't read Harley's mind. Who knows what's in there!" Katana quipped.

When Miss Martian began to laugh, Katana joined in, adding, "You know, you're pretty special. Harley can see that . . . and so can I."

Miss Martian glowed when she heard this. She looked at Katana and said, "So are you." She paused and took a breath. "Katana, there's something you were born to do, something deep inside you waiting to happen—something big."

Katana felt a chill run through her. This wasn't like when Frost blasted her in Wildcat's class, or when Captain Cold tried to freeze her at Capes & Cowls. No, this was different, and she wasn't sure if it was good or bad.

"What is it?" Katana asked.

Miss Martian shook her head. "I don't know," she admitted. "It's weird, but I'm getting impressions from an outside source. Like there's a thought that is patiently waiting until the right moment to make itself known to you."

"An outside source?" Katana echoed. "I don't understand."

"Nor do I," said Miss Martian. "However, I sense that something unavoidable will happen soon and you're at the center of it."

Katana knew that people assumed she was strong and self-assured. A take-charge kind of girl. Wonder Woman and Supergirl were always saying this. Sometimes she felt empowered by their confidence in her. But like everyone, Katana sometimes had her doubts, especially at night.

Back home when she was young, Katana's parents worked late hours, as teachers often did. Though she loved them dearly, Katana didn't mind this at all, since it meant that her Onna would be there to take care of her. Both loved this special time.

Now, with only memories of her grandmother, Katana's thoughts raced back and forth—from the past to the present. She recalled the days of her youth, learning to wield her sword under the tutelage of the world's best—and then rushing forward to Super Hero High and the swords that had somehow presented themselves to her—for what? To store? To use? To protect?

Katana tried to stay awake when thinking about these questions, because falling asleep meant that the strange bad dream could come again. The one where an unseen shape was chasing her, catching her, and then . . .

Katana's own cries always awakened her before she could see who was after her. It was bad enough that she had this nightmare, but what was worse was that now she was thinking about it in the daytime, too.

In her spare time, which was not much with the Legacy project looming, Katana had taken to visiting the swords. She liked picking them up and trying them all out, lunging, swinging them over her head, and parrying. This was good practice. There was an opening for captain of the fencing team at Super Hero High, and Katana was set on getting it.

The swords were so fancy compared to the one Onna had given her. Katana wondered if one of these could make her better in battle. Each was an individual work of art, and some were so ornate they would not have been out of place in an art gallery or museum. Katana considered bringing some to Ms. Moone's art class to show her teacher. It was a shame, she thought, that the swords were locked away.

"It's probably nothing," Star Sapphire said. She was paired up with Katana for Waller's pet project, Team Clean, where

Supers tried to learn more about each other as they helped clean up Metropolis.

The teens were supposed to help with recycling and maintaining a clean city but usually created more of a mess. Today they were on loan for the purpose of cleaning Centennial Park—and to set good examples for the youthful citizens of Metropolis.

Star Sapphire levitated a battered old boot with a glowing light-construct glove from her power ring. While the boot was lifted by her violet energy, Sapphire still felt the need to hold her nose with her free hand. A few feet away, Katana speared some old newspapers with her short spear, called a te yari. Supergirl flew overhead carrying a dumpster, and Sapphire tossed the boot inside.

"Hey!" Beast Boy yelled. He stood up in the dumpster. "Watch where you throw things!"

"Thanks, Sapph," Supergirl yelled as she continued on. "Trash! Anyone got trash? Who's got trash?"

"One time, someone sent my mother a huge treasure chest," Star Sapphire told Katana. "It was sealed tight and took an army of mutant welders to laser it open."

"What was inside?" Katana asked. There were some empty bags of jalapeño potato chips scattered about. She speared them with her sword.

"Not much," Sapphire said, shaking her head. Her deep-purple-highlighted hair blew in the wind in slow motion, like something in a shampoo commercial. "Some old photos. A few trinkets. No gems or gold. Nothing of value."

"Well, maybe the things in them were of value to whoever once owned the chest," Katana mused.

"Exactly!" Star Sapphire said. "Those swords aren't really worth much to you. I mean, c'mon, it's like someone's asking you to store their old stuff."

Katana thought about this as they continued picking up trash. An old car left abandoned near the school, a bag of discarded bomb casings, some stale pizza. Maybe, she thought, the swords were sent to her for a reason. Was she supposed to use them? All of them? That wouldn't be possible for one person to do.

"Swords!" Miss Martian declared.

They were in Lucius Fox's Weaponomics class, and he had given them free time to work on anything defense-related. Katana had just buffed and polished her sword. To make sure her powers were in play, Star Sapphire kept pointing her purple ring at people and checking off their names when they smiled at her. Bumblebee was practicing her beesting blasts. Batgirl was refining her magnetic net caster. Cheetah was practicing her agility by dodging Wonder Woman's Lasso of Truth and Harley's heavy mallet.

"Swords!" Miss Martian said again.

"Is that right?" Poison Ivy asked Katana.

Katana nodded. She had been thinking about swords.

Mr. Fox walked up to Miss Martian. "How's it going?" he asked.

She gave him a small smile. "Good," she said, and then added, "But I'm still having trouble with my power. Sometimes I think I may be mind reading, when really I'm tracking random brain waves."

Mr. Fox nodded. "This is not uncommon," he assured her. "I had another student from Mars who experienced the same thing. But you're really progressing well. You'll get there."

Miss Martian blushed and said "Thank you" to Katana, who was thinking good thoughts about her.

"What am I thinking now?" Poison Ivy asked.

"That you could use more time for your science experiment?" Miss Martian said.

Ivy nodded.

"And me, what am I thinking?" Katana asked.

"Still swords," said Miss Martian. She giggled. "I wasn't reading your mind that time. You think about swords a lot."

She was right again. Katana could not get the swords off

her mind. But just then, she heard the strangest sound. She looked at Miss Martian, who covered her ears and scrunched her eyes shut.

Miss Martian whispered, "They're . . ."

"What is it?" Katana asked, wondering what the clicking noises were.

Others heard them, too. Everyone in Mr. Fox's class was either staring at Miss Martian or trying to find the source of the noise.

This time the shy green girl from Mars spoke up. "They're coming."

CHAPTER 14

"Who's coming?" Harley asked. She turned on her video camera and aimed it at Miss Martian. "What's that sound? *Everyone, quiet! We're trying to listen!*"

"Not now, Harley. I've told you before," Mr. Fox said patiently. Clearly, he had dealt with Harley Quinn before. The Weaponomics teacher inserted himself between the two of them, protecting the alien from Harley's oversized personality.

Leaning toward Miss Martian, Mr. Fox asked gently, "Can you tell me what's going on? Are you reading someone's mind right now?"

Miss Martian shook her head. "I don't know what I'm getting," she said, putting her fingertips on her forehead and covering her face. "But whatever it is, it's getting closer."

Just then there was a crash in the hallway, followed by Parasite howling, "Get away!" Everyone could hear him swatting something with a wet mop. "Not in this school, you don't!"

As Katana and the others stuck their heads out the doorway, they could see the janitor flailing about with his mop and bucket. "I *just* mopped the floor," he said angrily, "and they ruined it!"

"Who ruined it?" Batgirl asked. She had taken an intense-vision magnifying glass out of her Utility Belt and was surveying the scene. As she scrutinized the area, she brought a detail into focus: little scratches that lit up red under the ultraviolet light of her magnifying glass.

"It was them," Miss Martian said, as if in a trance. "They've arrived."

Katana and the others looked down on the wet floor but didn't see anything.

"Critters!" Parasite said, grumbling. "Scrambling so fast, I couldn't really even see them."

"Was it a Parademon?" Big Barda asked, rushing down the hall. She looked hopeful. "I kinda miss them little critters."

"More likely it was a rodent," Beast Boy weighed in. "They're wily creatures." To prove his point, he turned into a green mouse and started chasing Frost, who hated mice so much that just the sight of one would cause a crack in her usually cool demeanor.

"Well, whatever it is, it's gone now, and it doesn't seem

to be a threat," Mr. Fox said, herding his students back into the classroom. "Frost, stop trying to blast Beast Boy with icicles. Beast Boy, stop being a mouse. Whatever it is, let's let Parasite deal with it."

Katana looked at Miss Martian, whose apologetic shrug said she had lost whatever vibe she had been getting. For everyone else, the episode had merely been an interesting diversion from class, but Katana couldn't help thinking that another mystery had just presented itself.

Though their schedules were packed with June Moone's art projects, Mr. Fox's weapons checks, Crazy Quilt's costume redesigns, Commissioner Gordon's forensics demonstrations, and Doc Magnus's computer assignments, the majority of Supers had Liberty Belle's Legacy project on their minds the most. Katana in particular.

"What do we know about Japan?" Liberty Belle asked.

Batgirl raised her hand. "Japan is a string of islands on the eastern edge of Asia. People arrived over thirty thousand years ago—"

Liberty Belle nodded after Batgirl went on for another five minutes, giving a broad history of the country. "Thank you, Batgirl. Now for a more personal perspective—Katana," she said. "Will you tell us a little bit about where you grew up?"

There was a scampering sound, like lots of tiny tapping. Liberty Belle ignored it. Teachers were experts at ignoring distractions. More and more, the sounds were being heard around the school. But no one could figure out what was causing it. Some teachers pretended not to hear it. Others, like Crazy Quilt, ran around trying to find the source of the sound. And Wildcat, the phys ed teacher, stomped and growled whenever the scampering was near.

"Ignore the noise," Liberty Belle said. "Katana, please go ahead."

"I was born in the Tottori prefecture," Katana said, smiling at the thought of her coastal village. "It boasts the largest sand dunes in Japan, and there's even a museum dedicated to sand sculptures. Up nearby Mount Kyusho are the Tottori castle ruins. I loved going there and seeing the entire city from up above."

As Katana continued telling her classmates about her hometown, others began to daydream about theirs, and some even got a little homesick. Liberty Belle smiled at Katana when she was done.

Big Barda leaned over to her and whispered, "I wish I was from Tottori. My homeland is Apokolips, and I never want to go back there!"

Supergirl couldn't help but hear the conversation. "Your

home is here with us now," she reminded Barda. "You don't have to go back."

Katana nodded in agreement. Apokolips was a desolate and unforgiving place. It was there that Granny Goodness had trained her army of Female Furies—Big Barda among them. But unlike the other Furies, Barda didn't want to conquer other worlds. She wanted to be a hero, and she was set on proving this at Super Hero High.

"May I have your attention, please?" a voice boomed.

All heads turned toward the video screen in the front of the room. Principal Waller's imposing frame filled the screen. "Supers," she began, "as most of you have figured out, we have some sort of critter problem at Super Hero High. It's more of a nuisance than anything else, but it's a distraction and a disruption we can't afford. Therefore, if any of you have any information or insight as to what the cause is, please let me know immediately!"

There was a lot of buzz in the room after Waller went offline. The biggest theory floating around was that the new tech wizard who had replaced Batgirl was to blame. Lena Luthor had turned out to be a villain. She had created Kryptomites and unleashed them on the school before she was found out and captured. The small, colorful annoyances could be quite destructive, and not all of them had been found.

In the halls outside Liberty Belle's classroom, Parasite was grumpier than usual after the announcement. The creatures that no one could see were driving him crazy. For a while he blamed Granny Goodness, the former librarian Supergirl, Batgirl, and the others had defeated in an epic battle.

"She probably left some of her Parademons behind to annoy me," he said to anyone who would listen.

Like the Kryptomites, the Parademons were small and had an appetite for destruction.

"If you catch one can I have it?" Big Barda asked. "I'll take good care of it, I promise!"

"You can have all of 'em!" Parasite said.

Barda beamed at the thought.

Granny had been responsible for the mischievous critters, but they had all been captured along with her, or so it was thought.

"Or . . . it could be mice or mini robots or those new snake-turtles everyone's talking about," Beast Boy said as he set the traps.

Harley was videotaping and getting in the way. "Tell me about this," she said as she stuck her finger in one of the traps, and yelped when it sprang on her.

Beast Boy puffed himself up and motioned to Arrowette and the others who were now helping him place the thin metal cages around the school. "I'm president of the FOW," he explained. "The Friends of Wildlife club—and we have a catch-and-release program. Once we capture the creatures, we'll find their natural habitat and return them!"

Still, with everyone on high alert, no one had seen the creatures, but they could hear them scattering about. Every now and then someone would say they caught a glimpse. . . .

"They're microscopic, and there are thousands of them!"

"They're small but have *huge* claws!"

"The sounds came from their rows of horrible teeth chattering."

"It's just one creature, like a centipede but with a thousand tiny horse hooves!"

Katana wished she could stop the noise. For whatever reason, it always seemed to follow her. At first she thought it was a coincidence. But later the Junior Detective Society ran some tests and discovered that the noise was indeed more prevalent whenever Katana was around.

"It's almost as if whatever it is, is trying to get your attention," Bumblebee told her after the JDS had finished their analysis.

Well, it has, Katana thought. *What now?*

CHAPTER 15

"Earth to Katana, Earth to Katana," Poison Ivy joked.

"Are you going to eat those?" Wonder Woman asked, pointing to the plate of sweet potato fries in front of her.

"Huh? Oh, sure, you can have some," Katana said. They were at Capes & Cowls Café, and Katana had been thinking about becoming the fencing team captain. Onna would have been so proud of her, if she got it.

Katana recalled her grandmother training her every day in swordsmanship. "Hold it like this," she had instructed Katana. "No need to grip it so tight. Be at one with your weapon."

"Hand it over!" someone yelled.

Suddenly, the silence cut through the café like a knife.

Steve Trevor looked stricken. Instantly, Wonder Woman was at his side. She lifted her shield in an effort to protect him from a large reptilian creature who had a bad habit of robbing banks, stores, and restaurants. Even across the café, Katana could see how the scaly behemoth's savage disposition had earned him the nickname "Killer Croc."

Batgirl reached for her Batarang. Katana put her hand on her sword. Big Barda gripped her Mega Rod.

"The money is in the safe . . . ," Steve Trevor insisted.

"I believe you," Croc hissed, grinning and showing his snaggleteeth. "But my friend here does not." He motioned to a huge gray humanoid shark who was snacking on the lunches Steve had just served to his customers.

"We are not having this conversation," Wonder Woman said. She looked at the patrons of Capes & Cowls, most of whom were cowering under the tables. "Steve, step away. I'll handle this."

"Listen, little lady," Croc said. His scaly skin looked like it needed moisturizer. "This is about the money, not you. So I suggest you scram before anyone gets hurt." He motioned to the oversized criminal with a sour look on his ghoulish face. "Isn't that right, Sharky, ol' pal?"

King Shark finished off a peach pie, then made his way toward them, leaving pools of seawater with each step. "This place is a dump!" he said, picking up a table and throwing it across the room. "Or at least, it will be when I'm through with it."

Before the table could hit a boy from Metropolis High,

Wonder Woman whipped out her Lasso of Truth and caught it just inches from his head, then swung it toward King Shark.

Croc laughed as he stood tall and swiped at a bin of forks and knives. The utensils flew with lethal speed around the room and stuck into the walls.

As the non-Super patrons started to scatter, Wonder Woman used her shield to protect them, while Barda tossed her Mega Rod at Croc's massive feet. The hurtling missile knocked the criminal's feet from under him and he fell toward Katana, who leapt out of the way. Suddenly, she heard someone whisper, "The sign," and looked up. *Yes! The Capes and Cowls neon sign,* she thought. She took aim at the chain that secured it to the ceiling and sliced the metal with her sword. Coming loose, the sign fell . . . hitting Croc. Stunned, he looked around and roared.

Stepping back, Katana took a deep breath and counted down, "Three . . . two . . . one!" With that, she sped forward with a series of front flips, kicking Croc in the chest with the final one. As Croc tumbled, Batgirl released a small amount of the reptile-repelling tear gas she had been working on. Croc's eyes swelled red as he began to wheeze and cough. Wonder Woman took the opportunity to wrap him in the Lasso of Truth. His big, bulky body crashed to the floor, totally tied up.

"What do you have to say for yourself?" she asked.

"I want to go home," Croc groaned.

"Too bad," Batgirl told him. "Because you're going to jail. *Pow!*"

On the other side of the café, King Shark was nursing a huge bump on the side of his head from where the table had hit him. "So sorry about that," Supergirl said.

Cyborg swept in as King Shark bared his sharp white teeth and lunged toward Supergirl. She flew out of his way just as he chomped down, biting Cyborg's metal arm instead of her.

Everyone in the room winced. That had to hurt.

"Please don't dent the metal," Cyborg said unflappably. "I was just buffed and polished."

As King Shark rubbed his aching jaw, Frost froze the brute to the jukebox, and Beast Boy turned into a polar bear and stood guard.

"You two villains picked the wrong place to rob," Cheetah said as she watched Wonder Woman work the room, making sure everyone was okay. She whipped out her phone and dialed 911. "Cheetah here. Yes, *that* Cheetah. I'm reporting an attempted robbery."

Before Cheetah hung up, the sounds of sirens blaring filled the air. Commissioner Gordon burst through the door, backed by Captain Maggie Sawyer and what looked like every single officer in Metropolis's Special Crimes Unit. He nodded to Batgirl and the others.

"Good work, Supers," he said.

"You're welcome," Beast Boy said, motioning to his fellow students. "Let's give everyone a round of applause!"

As the room erupted in cheers, Commissioner Gordon cuffed Croc and King Shark using mega-strength restraints his daughter, Barbara Gordon—and secretly Batgirl—had designed for the SCU.

"I'll be back!" King Shark threatened.

"Not if we have anything to say about it," Katana said.

Before he was out the door, Commissioner Gordon turned around and said, "The Metropolis Special Crimes Unit thanks you. We've been after this duo for weeks!"

The Supers smiled. It was always nice to hear praise, especially from a teacher who also happened to be a police commissioner.

"Everyone, be aware. Be safe. Be the best you can be," he said.

Katana looked at Wonder Woman, who was comforting a shaken Steve Trevor. "Thanks, Wonder Woman." He stood up. "Thanks to all the super heroes who captured the criminals, and to everyone at Capes and Cowls who didn't panic. Smoothies and carrot cake are on the house!"

The café was filled with chatter and laughter. Everyone was rehashing what had just happened—elaborating and embellishing their roles in the capture of the two wanted criminals. Wonder Woman and Supergirl had volunteered to help Steve serve the food to everyone, and what would have taken him an hour in multiple trips took only minutes with their help.

Katana sat back and nibbled on her carrot cake, content just to observe the crowd. Big Barda was being thanked by some of the restaurant's patrons. They seemed to be particularly impressed with her use of the Mega Rod. Though Barda looked uncomfortable with the praise, Katana could see that she was secretly pleased.

Batgirl was showing Arrowette her new tear gas, already talking about ways to increase its potency. "You never know when you're going to face reptile men in this town," she said, and Arrowette nodded in agreement.

Beast Boy was holding court in the middle of the room, asking if anyone wanted him to autograph their menu.

"This was an amazing show of teamwork," Lois Lane, teen reporter, said as she recorded the news flash for the *Daily Planet* site. "When it comes to saving lives, the teens from Super Hero High know what they're doing!"

Did she know what she was doing? Katana wondered. She wasn't even sure of what was going on in her own life. There was so much to think about. Some critters or something, who appeared harmless other than the constant and ever-growing distraction they caused, were following her around school. One hundred swords had found their way to her—or was it vice versa? And Katana could not get over the news of how her grandmother had perished. Who would want to do away with Onna, and why? *Why?*

"As super heroes," her grandmother once told a young Katana, *"our hours are not our own."*

"But why do you always have to leave me?" Katana had asked, pouting.

"I always come back," Onna assured her. *"I am always with you."*

"More cake?" Steve asked.

"Huh?" Katana shook her head, surprised to find herself still at Capes & Cowls.

"Sure, okay," a voice said across from her.

Katana noticed the empty plate. Miss Martian was now sitting at the table. "Thank you," she said to Steve. The alien took a big bite and smiled at Katana.

Katana smiled back. "You helped capture the criminals, didn't you?" she said.

Miss Martian nodded. "I merely read their minds and knew what their next moves would be, then whispered them to some of the Supers."

"The sign," Katana said as it dawned on her. "You pointed me toward the sign that I used to disable Croc."

When Miss Martian smiled, Katana knew she was right. She looked at Beast Boy and the others, who were still celebrating. "Why don't you take a bow?" she said.

Miss Martian shook her head. "Being a Super isn't about the glory," she replied. "It's about being able to help."

Katana gave her friend a hug. That sounded like something Onna would have said. She felt warmed by the memory of her grandmother, and smiled.

CHAPTER 16

"It's more of a bother than a crisis," Katana was saying. They were talking about the critters or the whatevers that seemed smitten with her.

Katana liked what Poison Ivy was wearing that day—colorful layers of chiffon that swayed as she walked and, as always, flowers in her flowing red hair. Katana preferred sleek, bold lines and functional black. Her grandmother's Samurai costume was like that. Though it was ornate and detailed, it conveyed strength and function.

Onna used to let Katana try on her uniform. The first time, she laughed at little Katana buried under the size and weight of the Samurai armor. It was so heavy she couldn't stand and fell over on her back, and her grandmother had to help her up.

"One day," Onna had said to an embarrassed and sobbing Katana, "you will be big and strong enough to wear this."

"But that is a long way off," a voice had said. Both looked up, surprised to see Katana's father standing in the doorway. "And besides, there's still a chance Katana will take after her mother and me and become a teacher."

Onna gave him a slight nod. "There are many ways to be a teacher," she had reminded her son-in-law. "Katana must follow her heart, as I did, and as her mother did, and as you did."

"Fair enough," her father had said before leaving. He nodded, but looked troubled.

"So we were thinking of a way to capture the critters," Bumblebee was saying. She was flying alongside Katana and Poison Ivy as they headed to Centennial Park to brainstorm. The expansive park was filled with citizens of Metropolis and students from the nearby schools. Beast Boy was visiting his friends at the zoo. Frost was freezing the lake so people could ice-skate, despite the warm weather. Picnic blankets quilted the ground as Frisbee players leapt over them, and Supers flew above.

"This looks like a good spot," Poison Ivy said. She unfurled her blanket as Bumblebee opened the wicker basket filled with sandwiches, cheeses, fruit, and, of course, honey.

"I'm thinking that the traps Beast Boy and the others have set are scaring away the critters," Bumblebee said as she poured a generous amount of honey over a thick slice of freshly baked bread from Butterwood's Bakery.

Katana had wondered about that herself.

"Maybe the critters are just shy," Poison Ivy said. She handed a cantaloupe and a honeydew melon to Katana, who tossed them in the air. She sliced the melons open and then carved them into bite-sized stars, crescent moons, and other shapes as Bumblebee held out a bowl and caught them. Poison Ivy added grapes to make the fruit salad and set aside the melon rinds for her organic garden's compost heap.

"So instead of scaring them away, what if we make a cozy, friendly place for the critters?" Poison Ivy said.

Bumblebee nodded and added even more honey to her bread. She took a bite, then said, "They have given us no indication that they aim to harm us. And it seems like they are quite taken with you, Katana. We think that if you are more welcoming, instead of always running away from them, maybe they will reveal themselves. They might be Kryptomites or Parademons, or something else entirely, but we won't know unless we stop guessing and start being proactive."

"We really do need to do something about them," Poison Ivy added. "You should have seen Vice Principal Grodd. He just got back from his annual vacation in Gorilla City and was all chill, until he heard the sounds of the critters running around. Then he instantly got back to his usual tense self! He's so wound up, Grodd's been passing out detention slips for Supers being *too quiet*. He would rather put up with *our* noise than hear the sounds of the critters."

Katana had seen the effects the creatures had been having. Though they were small and most likely harmless, it was like when there was a renegade fruit fly in the room and that was all you could pay attention to. Just that morning in Flyers' Ed, there had been a midair collision when Supergirl's super-hearing keyed in on the critters rather than teacher Red Tornado.

Katana bit into a butterfly-shaped piece of honeydew melon. It was sweet and juicy and as good as any candy she had ever eaten. She thought about her friends' suggestion. It had not occurred to her to face the critters. But why not? What did she have to lose?

The next day in Ms. Moone's art class, Katana listened for the familiar sound of the creatures. But instead, all she heard was the teacher talking about art imitating life—or was it the other way around?

"There is art all around us," June Moone was saying as she weaved her way around the big tables where the Supers sat. She lifted her hoodie off her head. Katana admired the emerald barrette in her hair. "Yes, art is in sculpture, paintings, music, and more," her teacher continued. "But the way you approach battle, the way you fight for justice and save lives, there is an art to that, too. For today's assignment, I want you all to think about how your life informs your art and vice versa. Then we will meet in small groups and discuss."

It reminded Katana of Dr. Arkham's Family Business meetings. Though the weekly sessions had been helpful and made her feel better, they weren't helping her solve the mystery of the swords or the sounds. "You need to identify and address that which causes you stress," Dr. Arkham had recently told the group.

Katana was perplexed. Why the swords? What were the sounds? How could she address her stress if she didn't even know what it was?

The critters had stopped following Katana. Did they know she was going to try to engage them? As she walked down the corridors, she listened but heard nothing. Katana actually started to miss the familiar clicking noises.

There was a sign outside the gym. It read: FENCING TEAM CAPTAIN TRYOUTS. Katana pushed open the door. Cyborg, Arrowette, and Lady Shiva all looked up at her.

"Uh-oh, this tryout just got ramped up by one hundred," Cyborg said, nodding to Katana.

"I'm still game," Lady Shiva said, standing and stretching.

"Let's do this," Arrowette said. "Best of luck to everyone."

Katana surveyed her competitors, making a note of each one's special skills. "Yes, good luck, everyone," she said, and she meant it. Though she badly wanted to be team captain, Katana also wanted to earn the spot.

The competition was fierce. Things like this usually were with the Supers. But in the end, even though Arrowette had deadly accurate aim, Lady Shiva had all the right moves, and Cyborg had the skills and strength, it was Katana who was clearly the best person for the job. She embodied everything her peers did, and more.

"Congratulations, Katana," Wildcat said. The others tried to look thrilled for her. "You are our new fencing team captain!"

"Um, I have a list of reasons why I'd be perfect for this," Katana said, taking a piece of paper that she had tucked into the folds of her costume. "I've also developed a series of fencing strategies and exercises for the team."

"I don't think you heard me," Wildcat said. "You got the job, Katana! It's not going to be easy; we're low on swords and our next shipment isn't due for another month or so. Plus, the team is somewhat new, so there's a lot of intensive training to be done. But if you're up for leading, you're it!"

Katana nodded enthusiastically. This was something she knew she could do.

Katana felt light as she made her way back to the dorms. *Fencing team captain!* She couldn't wait to tell her parents. They would be so proud. That was when she heard it—the clicking! The creatures were suddenly back! She slowed and the sounds slowed. She sped up and so did they. As planned, she made her way outside to Harmony Garden.

Poison Ivy had surrounded it with a tall hedge but had created a secret opening known only to her, Bumblebee, and Katana. They had figured a meditative place like the garden might be just the thing to lure whatever was making the sound. Not a trap, just a place to *be*.

Katana accessed the opening. Once inside, she was surrounded by lush plants and colorful, fragrant flowers. It was welcoming and safe. Slowly, Katana sat down on the soft green grass.

"Do you want to tell me who you are?" she asked.

There was a slight rustling behind some of the bushes.

"It's okay," Katana said, like Poison Ivy and Bumblebee

had suggested to her. "You're safe here."

Silence. All she could hear was some laughter from beyond the garden as Supers made their way across campus. Katana realized that the critters were gone again. She was alone. Had she made them nervous? Had she scared them away? As Katana started to get up, she was startled to see some leaves walking toward her.

CHAPTER 17

"Crabs?" Bumblebee said, looking tickled as she lifted one of the leaves that was milling about. "They're so cute!"

"They look sort of angry," Poison Ivy noted, peering down at them and waving hello. The little creatures remained camouflaged under their leaves, but she got the sense that they acknowledged her.

Katana stared at the small crabs staring back up at her. They were only slightly bigger than her fist. She had heard about these. Onna had told her about Ghost Crabs, "Always present, seldom seen," but Katana had always thought they were just another one of her grandmother's stories. Onna had told her so many stories: of dragons that flew, of crabs that talked, of battles, of victories, of defeats.

When Katana was researching her Legacy project, Liberty Belle had suggested that she look into Japanese myths and legends. Katana learned that there were feuds that lasted generations, but things like warring families turning to stone were just stories. She learned that the legendary Invincible Sword—also called the Muteki Sword—had never been found. And she learned that the legend of the Ghost Crabs dated back to the days of the Samurai and had mythical implications. But thinking they weren't real, Katana had eventually stopped her research to focus on her grandmother's real-life exploits as a Samurai super hero.

She bent down and spoke to the shimmering crab that appeared to be the most forward and fearless of them. "Are you here to meet me?"

The crab discarded its leaf and gave her a slight nod with its whole body.

"We won't hurt you," Poison Ivy promised.

"Look!" Bumblebee said. There was awe in her voice.

All around them, plants began to rustle. One by one, more and more Ghost Crabs appeared. Each was different, with the face of what looked like a warrior on its shell. They stood at attention, all lined up in ten rows, ten abreast.

"I think they're trying to tell you something," Poison Ivy said. "But what?"

Katana shook her head. She wished Miss Martian were here. Maybe she could help. Katana knelt down and was about to talk to them when the alarms sounded.

"SAVE THE DAY DRILL! SAVE THE DAY DRILL! SAVE

THE DAY DRILL!" blared over the public address system.

"I gotta go help get the word out," Bumblebee said, instantly flying away and calling out, "Save the Day drill!"

Katana watched her leave, then turned back to the Ghost Crabs. But they had disappeared!

If Poison Ivy and Bumblebee had not seen them, too, Katana would have thought it was just her overactive imagination after so much research into Japanese history and lore. As much as she wanted to, there was no time to look for the crabs while the Save the Day alarm was still ringing.

"What do you think we'll have to do this time?" Hawkgirl asked Katana. She was flying over the mountains toward the ocean. Alongside her, Katana was testing out one of the prototype jetpacks Batgirl was working on in Mr. Fox's class. The Save the Day drills gave the Supers a chance to practice their skills, test out new weapons, flex their powers in real-life situations, and see how they would react in a crisis.

"Huh?" Katana said. She had been thinking about the Ghost Crabs. Why were they at Super Hero High? And what did they want with her?

Katana adjusted the straps on her jetpack. She loved that

Batgirl was always coming up with new technology to aid the Supers. Katana hoped the battery was fully charged. She had seen what happened to Cyborg when his power was low.

Starfire, another student from a distant world, and Supergirl were soaring alongside them. As they veered off toward the desert, Supergirl yelled, "Next stop, Sedona, Arizona! Good luck, you two!"

Hawkgirl and Katana waved back.

Some Save the Day drills utilized the powers of the full student body in one exercise, like the time all the teachers and staff were placed at the edge of a volcano—albeit an inactive one that Waller had filled with bubbling red goo. It was up to the Supers to rescue them in under an hour. But then there were actual Save the Days, like last month when the teens were charged with relocating a small village in the Alps during a massive landslide. When the goats refused to move, Beast Boy turned into a yeti and herded them to safety.

Today's Save the Day drill was a two-person-team exercise. Each duo was given an assignment, and they fanned out east, west, north, and south. "Remember," Waller instructed. "I am challenging you to think outside the box! Yes, use your special skills and powers, but also employ some creativity. And remember, *teamwork!*"

Katana could smell the ocean before she could see it. The salty sea air reminded her of home. The Supers passed a mass of seagulls flying in the opposite direction. In the distance, past the forest was a rolling ocean of waves.

"Over there!" Hawkgirl called, pointing.

Katana squinted and then saw him. It was Parasite, sitting on a wooden raft bobbing up and down on the waves. He looked annoyed at having to participate in the exercise. When he saw them circling above, he shouted, "Well, it's about time you got here."

Without warning, the sun disappeared behind black storm clouds. Lightning struck and thunder boomed as water poured from the sky. The ocean bucked like a bronco as the waves thrashed around, sending the raft up in the air and then slapping it back down on the water.

"Help me!" Parasite yelled. This time he was serious—and his normally purple face became tinged with seasick green. "Save me!" was the last thing Katana heard before Parasite was hit by a wave as tall as the Amethyst Tower. Instantly, the raft shattered and he disappeared under the turbulent surface.

CHAPTER 18

Without hesitating, Katana ditched the jetpack midair and plunged headfirst into the ocean. She was glad that years of swimming and surfing back home had prepared her for this.

The rain was relentless. Hawkgirl caught the jetpack before it hit the water and secured it around her waist. Then she readied a rescue rope and harness and got into position.

Over and over, Katana dived under the water in search of Parasite. At first the cold sea seemed murky, but soon her eyes adjusted. Above the surface the storm was unrelenting; however, there was a calm under the waves. The serene silence was at odds with the tumult each time Katana shot up and broke through to the surface to catch her breath.

"Do you have him?" Hawkgirl would call out above the thunder.

Katana just shook her head.

She dived deeper and deeper. She was glad that not being

too far from the coast, the water was not as deep as it might have been farther out. At one point Katana finally touched the bottom of the ocean. The sand was soft, and she thought she saw a Ghost Crab scampering to safety under a colorful coral reef.

But where was Parasite?

On her fourth dive down, Katana heard a confusing sound wafting toward her. It was coming from a conch shell floating peacefully past. She reached for it and rose from the waves to listen.

> These Samurai swords
> Entrusted to Katana
> Prepare for battle.

What battle? Katana wondered. The battle to save Parasite?

As she listened to it again, she thought it said, "Over there, I see him over there!"

The familiar voice knocked Katana back to her senses. It wasn't the conch shell speaking—it was Hawkgirl. She was pointing toward the bobbing purple head of Parasite, who was waving frantically. Katana tucked the shell into her pocket and with strong determined strokes swam to the janitor just as he went under. When he didn't reappear, Katana took a deep breath and dived down for a final time.

Parasite looked unusually calm. Katana swam over to him and grabbed his hand. She motioned for him to follow her and swim to safety. He shook his head. That was when she realized . . . Parasite couldn't swim!

Katana tightened her grip on the panicked janitor, who now began thrashing. She held him tight and then, using all her strength, kicked upward. Crashing to the surface, both gasped as they ravenously inhaled the air. The rain continued to pound, but at least they could breathe. Hawkgirl tossed the rope down to Katana, who secured it around Parasite's waist and then gave her partner a thumbs-up.

Though the jetpack was drenched, it still worked. *Thank you, Batgirl,* Katana thought as they flew out of the storm and back to Super Hero High with Parasite in tow.

"Don't tell anyone," Parasite said as they passed back over the mountains. Though he didn't elaborate, Katana knew what he meant: that he couldn't swim.

"Your secret is safe with me," she assured him.

"What are you talking about?" Hawkgirl asked as they neared Super Hero High.

"Nothing," Parasite said. He wasn't happy to be dragged through the sky by two super hero girls. But the sun was shining and the ocean was far, far away. By now, everyone had dried off.

"I'm just glad you're safe," Katana said to him. "I doubt

when you were sent on this Save the Day drill anyone knew that the weather would turn on us."

Parasite grumbled, but then added, "Thank you, Katana."

Everyone was talking about their Save the Day drills.

"Raven and I saved Ms. Moone from the jaws of a giant snake," Beast Boy bragged.

"I saved Wildcat from a crack in the earth's tectonic plates that were about to crush him," Star Sapphire announced.

"I was there, too," Miss Martian said quietly.

"Starfire and I unearthed Crazy Quilt from several tons of boulders," Supergirl added as the two high-fived. "He was *not* happy about the dirt that got on his blazer."

Though the weird change of weather and Parasite's rescue were foremost in her mind, Katana's thoughts kept straying back to the Ghost Crabs. Had she really seen one under the water?

That night, as Katana slept, she dreamt of the turbulent ocean, and of Parasite. Well, it looked like Parasite, but somehow she knew it wasn't really him. He was beckoning her to follow him under the sea. When she did, Katana saw the Ghost Crabs. As they stood on the coral reef, they welcomed her with their claws waving as she began to swim toward them, but before she could get near them, they scattered until not a single one could be seen.

In that instant, the warm water turned cold, and the dream turned into a nightmare. Katana tried to swim to the surface. But something was holding her back. She tried in vain to escape. Something or someone was after her again. . . .

CHAPTER 19

"Why can't we use the swords?" Harley asked. It was hard to keep a secret at Super Hero High, and by now everyone knew that there was a cache of swords hidden under the school.

It was pizza day in the dining hall, and Katana had pineapple on her two slices. She shifted uncomfortably in her chair, not wanting to answer the question or have her lunch disturbed.

"Well, everyone wants to join the fencing team now that you're team captain, but there aren't enough swords to go around and there's a roomful of spares just sitting there. It's a no-brainer!" Harley said. To make her point, she hit her mallet on the table, causing the pizzas to spin in the air before landing back on their plates.

Hmmmm . . . it does make sense, Katana thought. The Ghost Crabs had disappeared as mysteriously as they had appeared, and with her Legacy project under control, she was free to focus on the fencing team. As it was, with the lack of swords to go around, Katana was forced to improvise. In addition to traditional fencing, she had begun to incorporate other martial arts. And then, when her teammates wanted to be challenged, she had introduced other kinds of swordplay, like Kendo and Mugai-ryu using wooden swords.

This had caught the attention of so many Supers, the fencing team was *the* team to be on.

"I want you to take the team to the next level," Coach Wildcat told Katana. They were in the gym moving the rock-climbing wall, being careful because some rocks were booby-trapped to give the exercise a degree of unpredictability. "We have quite a few members, as you know, and we're ranked among the best in our league. But I want to see how far the Super Hero High fencing team can go, and with you at our helm, who knows?"

Katana had always wanted to be team captain. It was a chance to use her sword skills to teach others and to bring honor to the school. When the news got out that she had been selected, sign-ups had skyrocketed, according to Batgirl, the official team statistician. Katana had felt pride—and pressure—when she heard. Supers were always up for new and fun ways to fight and test their skills. Plus, it went unsaid that they wanted to best the other fencing teams. The school had recently won the 100th Super Triathlon, beating the top schools from all over the solar system. Everyone knew that Super Hero High students were hardworking and competitive.

As Katana consulted her lists of fencing strategies and moves, she thought back to what her grandmother had taught her. Even as a child, Katana was always eager to fight and show off her skills. However, Onna was always reminding her to slow down. She didn't understand why, though. Wasn't faster better? Coach Wildcat was always pushing everyone to "Go faster!" and "Break the sound barrier!"

"Like this?" Cyborg asked as he lunged.

"Try to relax a bit more," Katana instructed him. She wondered if his metal ever caused him to have stiff joints or to rust.

"I've got it! Katana, look at me! Look at me!" Harley called out. She had a sword in one hand and was trying to record herself with the other. "I'm a natural!"

"She's a natural *something*," Frost said as she parried away from Cheetah, who was as graceful as she was lethal. Since there weren't enough swords to go around, Frost had improvised and was using an icicle.

"What about leaps?" Harley asked, jumping into the air and doing a back-to-front flip in the process.

"What *about* leaps?" Katana asked. She was adjusting Big

Barda's grip on her sword. "There's no need to hold it so tight," she told her. "You should be at one with your sword, not smash it."

"But what if I feel like smashing something?" Barda asked.

"Don't look at me!" Beast Boy yelped.

"Hmm, leaps?" Katana said, getting back to Harley's earlier suggestion.

When she'd taken the job as team captain, Katana hadn't realized how hard it would be. It seemed like everyone was trying to get her attention at the same time. Was this what the teachers had to go through? Was this what her parents had to contend with every day?

"Yes!" Katana cried, startling Supergirl, who was standing right next to her. "Let's do leaps and gymnastics, and other martial arts moves. Why not?"

"Because it's not a good idea?" Cheetah said. She was standing in the middle of the room looking fiercer than usual. "When are we going to get enough swords for everyone? I'm tired of sharing with her." She pointed to Poison Ivy, who was taking her turn with their shared sword as she cut, thrust, and parried with Lady Shiva.

Cheetah had a valid point. Katana realized that she had a lot of work to do to make this all happen. And having enough swords for her team was a big part of that.

By the time the next fencing team meeting arrived, the gym was packed with Supers. Word had gotten out that not only would they get phys ed credit for being on the team, but it was fun, too!

As Katana led the group in warm-up exercises, some Supers showed off by doing a thousand jumping jacks instead of a hundred. Others, when asked to lunge across the gym, lunged all the way across campus and back. But when it came time for actual swordplay, everyone got serious.

"Your sword is an extension of yourself," Katana instructed, trying to remember what her grandmother had taught her. "Fencing is a martial art. And there's emphasis on the word *art*."

June Moone watched from the back of the room and nodded as Wildcat stood with his arms crossed, taking note of who was doing what—but most of all assessing Katana. By then, everyone had heard of the amazing job she was doing with the team.

"Line up!" she ordered.

In a nanosecond, the Supers were in straight rows. "Put your swords down," Katana said. "Now walk away from them." There was grumbling and a few complaints, but they did as they were told. "Now, back to your weapons!" Katana shouted, and they ran quickly to reclaim their swords. "Take your stance!"

The Supers smiled as they gripped the handles of the swords. Each person's stance was different—unique. Some, like Cheetah, crouched impossibly low, looking ready to strike. Others, like The Flash, looked quick and . . . flashy. And still others, like Bumblebee, were agile and light. As much as Katana was teaching her peers about fencing, she was learning about their individual styles—and learning to appreciate them.

By now, Katana was creating a new kind of sword fighting that combined martial arts, saber, foil, legend, and superpowers. With each training session she let her imagination take hold, determined to use each Super's skills to their best advantage.

June Moone smiled at Katana as she left the gym. "Art is everywhere," she could be heard saying. "It is a part of you."

"I guess it would be okay?" Katana said to the Junior Detective Society.

"I don't see why not," The Flash said. "And that part of

the haiku about battle . . . I think it means we're supposed to be prepared."

They were in the underground sword room. It was dark and cool. The weapons stood at attention as Batgirl counted. "Still one hundred," she announced. "All accounted for!"

"The fencing team needs them—we have so many members," Katana said, trying to convince herself. "No one is fond of using a pretend sword. Well, okay, Harley, but that's because she can pretend her mallet is a sword."

"It'll be okay," Poison Ivy spoke up. She admired a sword with an inlaid pearl handle of flowers intertwined with vines.

"I'm not so sure," Hawkgirl said. "We don't know why these are here." Just then she noticed a sword with a majestic hawk carved into the teak handle and embellished with gold. "Although, maybe it's all right." She picked up the sword and held it aloft. "What if we just use them for the fencing team and then return them every day after?"

"It's easy enough to take a daily inventory," Batgirl said. "I can put micro monitors on the swords and create a computer program to keep track of them at all times."

The Flash was already gathering them. "Fun with fencing!" he exclaimed as he began to take off.

"Stop!" Hawkgirl warned, flying after him. "You know that you're not supposed to run with sharp pointy objects!"

Katana couldn't think of a reason not to use the swords. Maybe, just maybe, that was why they'd been sent to her. Though the fencing team was gearing up for competition against other high schools, everyone knew that the skills they were learning would translate to battle, should it come to that.

And quite frankly, if the swords were not going to explain their purpose, then she was going to give them one.

Remember the haiku, Katana told herself.

> *These Samurai swords*
> *Entrusted to Katana*
> *The story unfolds.*

> *These Samurai swords*
> *Entrusted to Katana*
> *Prepare for battle.*

"Okay," Katana said. "Swords for everyone."

CHAPTER 20

A cheer went up as Katana—followed by The Flash, Bumblebee, Hawkgirl, and Batgirl—entered, carrying a hundred swords. By then the gym was full. Luckily, this time there were enough swords to go around. Team members were each assigned one as Batgirl logged it into a database. Everyone was thrilled to be in possession, however temporary, of the beautiful Samurai weapons.

"Supers, get ready," Katana announced as she did a triple backflip, followed by a series of roundhouse kicks. "You're going to learn swordsmanship like no one's ever seen before!"

As she led the team exercises, Katana thought she saw something out of the corner of her eye.

The Ghost Crabs were back.

Earlier, with Batgirl's help, they had been able to look up several articles about the mythical creatures, and had even unearthed some ancient cave paintings of them. But that was all they could find. It was as if the Ghost Crabs chose to be invisible. And yet, here they were.

Katana spied them watching from the bleachers with quiet approval.

"Look at me!"

A green swordfish holding a sword bounced on its tail past Katana.

"Beast Boy, stop that!" she ordered. "You need to respect your sword, it is not a toy!"

A chastened Beast Boy turned back into a teenager and muttered, "You're no fun," before quickly regaining his good-natured disposition.

Katana turned back to where the Ghost Crabs had been, but they were gone. Disappointed, she returned to teaching her peers about how to respect and handle their swords. She had thought that maybe the Ghost Crabs had gone into hibernation, or had gone home, wherever that was.

Not knowing what to make of them, Katana figured they were just somehow drawn to her.

"Remember when that flock of parrots flew alongside me for three days in a row?" Hawkgirl said.

"Bats like me, and it's mutual," Batgirl mused. "I wonder where Batty is now?" she added, thinking of the adorable baby bat she had befriended a short while ago.

"Kittens love me," Cheetah had told her. "Can you blame

them? I'm their role model."

Katana sat alone in the bleachers and turned her focus from the Ghost Crabs to the very real fencing team, who were working hard, practicing, practicing, practicing. She had named Cyborg, Arrowette, and Lady Shiva as her assistants, and they were doing a terrific job. Still, Katana wished her grandmother were with her. Onna could have told her if she had done the right thing by using the swords for the school's fencers. She could tell her what the conch shells meant.

> *These Samurai swords*
> *Entrusted to Katana*
> *The story unfolds.*
>
> *These Samurai swords*
> *Entrusted to Katana*
> *Prepare for battle.*

Her friends discussed the possible meanings.

"The battle of good versus evil?" Hawkgirl asked.

"The battle for humanity?" said Poison Ivy as she passed out fragrant roses in bloom.

"The battle for the best fencing team?" The Flash suggested.

"The battle of determining who we are?" said Batgirl, looking up from her portable computer.

The Junior Detective Society was meeting to discuss the latest haiku. Katana had set the two conch shells on the table. All stared at the shells as if they were the answer, when really, to Katana, they were the questions. Her mind drifted back to her grandmother.

"You ask so many questions," Onna had said, pulling her granddaughter close for a hug.

"I am sorry," young Katana said, smiling because she knew that Onna would always give her an answer, or a story that seemed to contain an answer.

Onna stepped back and put her hands on Katana's shoulders. "Seeking the answers is always admirable. Those who ask are open to knowledge. Those who do not, presume."

Gathered around Batgirl's computer, the Junior Detective Society was trying to parse the haikus by using a poetry analysis program. But as with the other attempts to pull meaning from the spare words, they had made little progress and kept circling without finding the center.

Katana leaned back in her chair and thought about home. She was grateful to her parents for keeping Onna's legend alive with stories about her career as the first female Samurai super hero. They had been telling her more to help with her Legacy project, and she was making a lot of progress.

Katana let her mind drift back to a recent conversation.

"Like you, Onna had quite an imagination," her mother said as they began their weekly AboutFace on-screen talk. *"She tried to shield me from some of her more dangerous missions, so I never knew what was real and what was not."*

"Was she in danger a lot?" Katana asked.

Her mother looked away. *"I think maybe. I was just a girl when I discovered who my mother really was. I worried for her all the time, just as I worry . . ."*

She didn't have to finish her sentence. Katana knew what she was thinking. *"Mom, I promise to do all I can to keep safe."* Her mother nodded unconvincingly. *"That's why I am here at Super Hero High,"* Katana said brightly, hoping her mother would catch her enthusiasm. *"I'm at school to learn. To practice. To become the best super hero I can be!"*

Her mother nodded again, then finally spoke. *"Tatsu, my daughter, you are an only child, just as your Onna was, and as am I. I just want what any mother wants—for her daughter to be happy and to be safe."*

"I am happy," Katana assured her. *"And I thank you and Dad for giving me this chance to learn and to honor Onna in the best way I know how. But I want to know more."* She paused, then corrected herself. *"I need to know more. It would help me in my journey to become a super hero."*

Her mother looked resolved. *"There are some things of*

your grandmother's that you may find of interest," she said. "I will send them to you."

"The battle to end all battles?"

"The battle with one's self?"

Katana came back to the moment and rejoined her friends in the conversation. "Maybe it means the battle for the last piece of Superfood Cake in the cafeteria."

They looked at each other. Grins spread across their faces. After a moment's pause, everyone dashed out of the room, laughing and squealing.

One morning a couple of days later, Katana found a wooden crate outside her room just as she was headed to class. Inside, wrapped in layers of padded cloth, was a red-lacquered teak chest. Katana ran her fingers over her grandmother's name. It was carved into the top and written in Japanese.

Slowly, she lifted the lid. It creaked slightly as a familiar scent wafted upward. Katana instantly recognized the smell as that of the Japanese snowball, a flower her grandmother had always loved. The flowers were plentiful in the woods near their house, and Katana could imagine her grandmother closing her eyes and inhaling its sweet perfume. The box was filled with the dried petals of the flower.

The first thing she found was a brown leather high school yearbook. A gold embossed crest consisting of a star, a flame, and a lightning bolt was on the cover. Katana gently brushed the petals off it. There was no time to go through everything in the chest, so she tucked the yearbook under her arm and headed out to class. She would look at the rest that night, Katana decided, after fencing practice, when she could devote more time to it.

Katana glanced at the chest before closing the door to her room. What mysteries did it hold . . . or solve?

CHAPTER 21

"**Y**ou look alike!" Big Barda said as she turned the pages. Katana peered over her shoulder. She and Onna did look alike: The same determined expression on their faces. The same strong stance. The same twinkle in their eyes.

Katana took the yearbook back. Though it was two generations old, she marveled at how the students still seemed the same. There were awesome aliens, dangerous dragons, a variety of humans, and creatures of undetermined origin. There were clubs and awkward senior photos, and teachers who looked stern. At least this was real, Katana thought. She had heard so many stories from her grandmother that she wasn't sure what was fact and what was fiction.

"Can you tell me about her? I wish I had a real grandmother," Big Barda said wistfully. "I mean, Granny Goodness raised me, but she ended up being, you know, evil. *Sheesh,* I always wonder what it would be like to be raised by someone good. A real super hero."

Katana felt she needed to tell Onna's story as much as Big Barda seemed to need to hear it.

"Before I was born, everyone thought my mother would have a baby boy. Something about the way her stomach looked, and the fact that even then I was always kicking. But since I was a girl, my parents named me Tatsu Yamashiro—Yamashiro being my grandmother's side. She was the last in a line of the Samurai legacy in her family, and with no boys to carry on the family name, the honor was bestowed upon me.

"I was a happy but intense child, and curious about everything, especially my grandmother's swords," Katana continued.

"'Careful, Tatsu,' Onna was always saying. 'You may hold my Katana sword, but only if I have my hands around yours.'

"The first time I held the sword, I couldn't stop smiling. Even though it was way too big for me, it was as if I had just been reunited with an old friend." Katana absentmindedly touched her sword. "'Katana!' my grandmother said, laughing. 'We should call you Katana.'

"And from that day forward, everyone called me Katana," she said, looking off into the distance.

"It's a really good name," Big Barda said. "So you were named after your sword? I wonder if I should tell people to call me Mega Rod."

"Barda is a beautiful name," Katana said. She began looking at the yearbook again. She stopped on a page that had her grandmother's photo on it. She was sitting between a small, skinny dragon and a girl with wide white wings.

"Wow, you really think so?" Barda asked.

"Think what?" Katana said. The photo had distracted her.

"That my name is a nice one."

Katana nodded. "The name is nice and so are you."

"Thanks, but don't let that get around," she said, punching Katana lightly on the shoulder.

"You have my word on that, *Mega Rod*," Katana replied. And the two girls burst out laughing.

That night Katana couldn't eat dinner fast enough. While sisters Thunder and Lightning were in a heated discussion over their Legacy projects, and Beast Boy, Cyborg, and The Flash were goofing off, Katana was eating her veggie lasagna as fast as she could. She was in such a hurry she ignored the thick slice of pineapple upside-down cake on her tray.

"You going to eat that?" Big Barda asked as she dug into her mountain of mashed potatoes.

"It's all yours," Katana said, handing her cake over. Barda beamed.

"Will you be joining our book club tonight?" Batgirl asked as Katana pushed her chair away from the table. "We're going to be discussing that new book about Shakespeare in the Fifth Dimension."

"Sorry, there's something I have to do," Katana said, brushing past Adam Strange. He had just adjusted his jetpack and was now flying around the room passing out homemade Moon Cakes that his grandmother had sent him.

"Katana," he called. "Catch!"

She leapt high in the air, caught the Moon Cake, tucked into a twirl midair, and continued running without breaking her stride all the way to the dorms.

After the hustle and bustle of the dining hall, Katana's room was blissfully quiet. She closed the door behind her and pulled the red teak chest into the middle of the room. Katana stared at it, wondering what she would find. Slowly, she raised the heavy lid of the chest. She was once again met with the sweet scent of snowball flowers. Inspired by Batgirl, Katana took inventory of what she found, including the yearbook:

1. High school yearbook from senior year

2. Snowball petals, dried and scattered

3. Articles about famous Samurai super heroes

4. Letters from Onna's parents telling her to be careful

5. Framed senior portrait of Onna looking strong, staring at the camera while wearing armor with a fresh snowball flower on top of the helmet

6. Misc. photos of Onna with friends—a group of girls, some alien, other earthlings, grinning; fencing team photo, with caption ONNA-BUGEISHA YAMASHIRO AND DRAGON PRINCE LEAD RED PLANET PREP TO VICTORY

7. Assorted weapons

8. Red silk kimono

Katana pulled her sleek black hair into a bun and secured it with a hairstick. She sat on the floor taking small bites of Adam Strange's Moon Cake as she lingered over the photos. High school! Everything was from when Onna was her age—when her grandmother was training to be a super hero at Red Planet Prep.

Onna looked so young. Her grandmother was co-captain of the fencing team? Why hadn't Katana known that? She wished Onna had talked more about herself. Katana examined the photo with the skinny kid called Dragon Prince standing next to her grandmother. He looked supremely uncomfortable. Both were holding their swords. Onna stood tall and looked straight at the camera, while her co-captain was looking at her.

As she read the articles, Katana learned more about the Samurai—and that when the reign of the Samurai ended, many did not know what to do with their lives. Some went into business, others took up other family trades like pottery and farming, a handful became super heroes—and though Onna could not have known it at the time, she would join their ranks.

Katana lifted up the kimono and held it in front of her. The red silk was shiny and there were delicate patterns embroidered with gold thread around the collar. A scene of an ocean was repeated on the robe. It was heavier than it looked.

Opening the kimono, Katana slipped into it. It wrapped around her like a robe. The garment fell to her ankles, and when she stretched her arms out, the kimono made a thick T-shape. Katana secured the obi, a kind of sash, in the back and regarded the image of herself in the mirror. She lifted her arms but noticed that one side was heavier than the other. Curious, Katana felt the long sleeve that draped halfway down the kimono. There was something inside it.

CHAPTER 22

The small black book was secured shut with a bronze latch. Katana flipped the latch open. It made a satisfying clinking sound. Inside the leather cover, Katana recognized her grandmother's handwriting. How could it be delicate and strong at the same time? On the first page it read: *Private property of Onna-Bugeisha Yamashiro!!! Keep out!!!*

Katana had to laugh. Her own diary had a similar warning on it. Wondering if she should continue, Katana paused. It seemed wrong to read something so personal that someone else had written. Yet, at the same time, this was her invitation to get to know her grandmother even better. She made up her mind and began to read . . .

Hello, Diary! I am honored and excited to have been accepted to Red Planet Prep. Everyone says it's one of the best super hero high schools

*in the universe! Though it's small, it has a
reputation for graduating great super heroes.
If I can make it all four years, I shall be
among those ranks.*

*It may seem petty for me to mention this,
because everything else is going so well, but
my roommate is causing me stress. She has
the annoying habit of flying in her sleep, which
means we have to keep the windows shut
at night, lest she fly away to who knows
where. But when she bumps against the walls,
I can't sleep—and our teachers keep telling
us that because we work so hard in the day,
we need to sleep hard at night. Plus, I am used
to sleeping with the windows wide open and
miss the fresh air and sea scent.*

Katana laughed at the thought of a sleep-flying roommate
and was glad that she had her own room. Everyone did
at Super Hero High, although they shared common space
where the rooms connected. Katana kept reading, eagerly
turning the pages.

Onna had many of the same fears and challenges that

Katana had—like fitting in and doing well at school. Though Onna had written:

> Some of the other students don't like it that girls are here. Red Planet Prep was a boys-only school for the longest time. But we're here to change that!

This was a new idea to Katana. She couldn't even imagine Super Hero High being all boys—or all girls.

Later, in other passages, Onna would go on to write:

> Am I homesick? Yes, I must admit I am. Father sends me letters three times a week and each one says the same thing: "I am so proud of you, Onna. Because you are an only child, you will be carrying on the legacy of the Yamashiro name. And as a super hero? The first female Samurai super hero? You bring such honor to our family.
>
> Your mother, of course, worries about your safety all the time. I admit, I do, too, but we both are behind you and wish you love. Speaking of which, have you found love at the school? Your mother and I met in high school! Papa.

Not much had changed since her grandmother was in high school, Katana noted.

As the sun set and the stars came out, Katana kept reading. There were larger issues, too, she discovered.

Why is being the first at something so difficult? There are those who aim to dissuade me from being a Samurai super hero. They say that a girl cannot do that—she is not strong enough, physically or mentally. Well, I am here to prove them wrong! Still, I must admit, their reservations, sometimes loudly vocal, are wearing on me. Most come from outside the school. There's a reporter who's keen on chronicling our lives, and he's penned several editorials asking, "A girl Samurai? A girl Samurai super hero? What is she thinking?"

Well, here's what I'm thinking—it's about time! It's about time there was a female Samurai super hero. I know that there have been others who have tried before me. But they were talked out of it, or even asked to leave their training academies. I sometimes forget how hard others have fought to allow us the liberties we have now. It is my dream to succeed, or at the very least make my dream a reality for someone else.

Katana stopped reading. Her heart was racing. She had just taken for granted that she would follow in Onna's footsteps. Though she knew that her grandmother was a first, Katana had never considered what she had gone through to achieve this honor.

A knock on the door startled Katana out of her thoughts. "Come in!" she called out.

"Hey, just wondering if you wanted to join our Legacy project work session," Bumblebee asked. She was holding a jar of honey in one hand and a photo album in the other.

"Thanks," Katana said. "But I'm working on it right now and would sort of like to be alone."

"Okay, sure. Later, then," Bumblebee said. Before she left, she said, "Nice kimono!"

Katana had forgotten she was even wearing it. The silk felt soft against her skin, and knowing that Onna had worn this when she was her age made it even more special. Once the door closed, Katana returned to the diary. When she got to the part about selecting their weapons, Katana read with a keen interest. She had the Katana sword her grandmother had gifted her, of course. But there were other weapons as well. Mr. Fox always told his students that they should never rely on just one weapon, power, or strategy in battle.

Katana put the diary down and looked at the weapons that had been in the chest. There was a heavy kusari-fundo, a weighted chain made of metal. Katana stood and circled it over her head, the way she had watched Wonder Woman do with her lasso. The ninja stars were smaller than the ones she had, but Katana noticed that Onna's were sharper. She set them aside—they would make a great addition to her weaponry.

In her own arsenal Katana counted a variety of knives of different sizes, a couple of spears, and her beloved tsubute, a stone-club throwing missile that Batgirl had supercharged by adding an electrified tip. There was also her blowgun, complete with knockout darts. Mr. Fox always made sure that Katana had a good supply of these. But Katana's sword was her weapon of choice; after all, she had been named after it.

In her diary, Onna had written of this very sword:

I love my Katana. It is sleek and simple, but serves me well. Or is it I who serves it? In fencing, Dragon Prince often makes fun of me for loving it so much. He says, "Are you going to marry it?" He's so funny, though not when I beat him in fencing!

I am grateful that my family supports my goal to become a super hero. Dragon Prince's father, the King, chides him at every opportunity. And whenever his father hears that he has lost another fencing match to me, Dragon Prince broods for days. "I lost to a girl," he says bitterly.

"We are friends," I always tell him. "And we battle as such. We learn from our losses and get stronger each time."

He is full of excuses, though.

"The sun was in my eyes."

"My sword is not as balanced as yours."

"I ate too much at lunch."

And I have to laugh. There is no excuse for not doing your best and being open to learning. When one ceases to learn, what is left?

CHAPTER 23

"What does he think of me?" Star Sapphire asked Miss Martian. She was looking across the room at the Green Lantern, Hal Jordan, who was about to bite into a sandwich the size of his head. Her curiosity seemed idle, but her ring glowed warmly on her finger regardless.

"That's not the sort of thing I use my powers for," Miss Martian said quietly but firmly.

Green Lantern looked up from his dinner, and when he saw Sapphire staring at him, he grinned—not realizing that Sapphire's ring was emanating a friendly vibration-wave in his direction—just as Beast Boy walked between the two of them.

"Wow! I feel warm and fuzzy," Beast Boy said as he was caught between the purple glow emitting from her ring and the power coming from Green Lantern's ring. "I *am* warm and fuzzy."

Star Sapphire rolled her eyes. "That wasn't meant for you," she said to Beast Boy, who was still wobbly as he made his way to join Animal Man and Silver Banshee at another table.

"Hey there!" Katana said, setting down her dinner tray. Fencing practice had gone particularly well that day, and she was pleased with everyone's progress. "You don't mind if I sit here, do you?"

Miss Martian looked relieved to see her. "Please have a seat," she said, motioning to the chair.

"Listen," Star Sapphire said to Miss Martian before she left. "If you ever need a new spacecraft or *anything,* you could work for me. Okay?"

Miss Martian nodded, suspecting that there would be strings attached to any favors done by Star Sapphire. "Um, okay?" she said as they watched Star Sapphire return to her table in the center of the room.

"You're doing well sticking up for yourself," Katana said. She dug into her vegetable casserole. Tonight's was especially good since everything was fresh from the organic garden that Poison Ivy was overseeing on campus. Katana especially liked the mushrooms.

"Thank you," Miss Martian said. She looked up as other Supers joined them.

Katana was just about to say "You're welcome" when she

heard a familiar clicking coming from beneath the table. The Ghost Crabs were back! The Ghost Crabs remained a mystery, but even though they could still be very distracting, only Parasite seemed concerned. "Always running around just when I've mopped," he grumbled. "Pests, that's what they are. Pests!"

The crabs had started causing mischief, like running for cover and causing Supers to trip—and depending on the powers of the student they tripped, the results could be spectacularly destructive, causing Vice Principal Grodd and Parasite endless grief. "The crabs ate my homework" was not an excuse accepted by the faculty—except one time when the crabs tattered Cheetah's fashion project and Crazy Quilt declared the results to be a marvelous example of distressed couture.

It was as if they wanted attention. Yet whenever anyone tried to capture one, they escaped with incredible powers of speed and stealth. The only teen they seemed to show any deference to was Katana, and now they were following her around campus, marching in straight rows, albeit at a respectable distance. And they were certainly well behaved when they watched the fencing team practice with the swords Katana had found. It seemed like that was the only time they weren't scampering around.

When Katana saw them again, she realized that she had

actually missed the little creatures.

Katana had never had a pet before, though she had always wanted one. But her parents had insisted that pets were like family, and to have one meant you also had to have the time to devote to them. Katana was so bent on getting into Super Hero High that she seldom had any time for herself, much less for a pet. So instead, she had stuffed animals. These Ghost Crabs were the closest things she had ever had to pets.

It wasn't uncommon for Supers to have otherworldly pets, although they had to be registered with Waller, and then the pets had to prove themselves to be manageable. Just last month, Harley's monkey, Calliope, had to be sent to a training camp because it kept swinging from the overhead lights and ripping them from the ceilings. And Wonder Woman had an adorable riding kangaroo named Jumpa, but it proved to be too distracting, because everyone wanted to play with it rather than study.

Batgirl had taken care of an injured baby bat recently. Poison Ivy often had butterflies follow her around . . . though maybe those didn't count as pets. Bumblebee had fostered the most adorable honey bear until she found a home for him. And Starfire even had an alien silkworm named—what else?—Silkie.

"There's one now!" Harley said as the girls were clearing their dishes. She gave Katana one of her irrepressible grins.

"Hey, wanna see what I made? It's hilarious! I'm gonna get tons of hits when I post this."

Katana cringed as she watched on the small screen of Harley's camera. It was a clip of the Ghost Crabs scampering around the corner following her. Then the video ran backward and forward, backward and forward, set to lively music that made it look like they were dancing.

"Seriously, Harley?" Katana asked. She wasn't keen on being on Harley's Quinntessentials. Oh, sure, some of the other Supers loved being on the Web channel, and even courted it. But Katana, like her grandmother before her, took high school a tad more seriously.

"You're a natural!" Harley assured her. "And if you don't like this clip, there are plenty more I can make. Like how about one of you tumbling and leaping up to avoid squashing one of the little critters?"

Katana blushed. That did happen. They had been underfoot often. "No, no thank you, this one is just fine," she assured Harley.

"There you are!" Bumblebee said, flying over to them. She held a pink slip of paper in her hand. "Waller would like to see you in her office." She handed the summons to Katana.

"Ooooh, are you in trouble?" Harley asked. Her eyes twinkled—this could be a story. "I'll go with you!"

"I'll go alone," Katana said, standing her ground.

"Whatever Principal Waller wants to say to me is not for your video channel."

"Aw, you're no fun," Harley said, giving an exaggerated frown.

Before Katana could respond, Harley had run off. "What's that I see?" she asked, looking off in the distance. "Supergirl's sneaker laces are untied again, and Beast Boy is headed in her direction with a stack of condiment-slathered sandwiches he can't see over—this *can't* end well! Gotta go!"

"Katana, have a seat," Amanda Waller said. She motioned to the wooden chair across from her. There was the usual stack of folders and some confiscated weapons on the principal's desk—a goo blaster, a still-glowing cannonball, and a pair of sharpened metal boomerangs.

"Yes, ma'am," Katana said. Her parents had taught her to always respect her elders.

"These Ghost Crabs, what do you know about them?" Waller asked. She was not one for small talk.

"Not much," Katana admitted. "But I think they like me."

"Well, that much is evident," the principal noted. "We've had lots of incidents with fans—be they human, alien, or otherwise—following our students around. And that's what

I'm thinking the Ghost Crabs are. Fans of yours. And while it is flattering, it can become a nuisance. I'm going to have to ask you to have a talk with them."

"I'm supposed to talk to them," Katana told Miss Martian as they walked out of Liberty Belle's class. It was ironic, but when they were first assigned the Legacy project, Katana had wondered if she had enough information. Now she was overloaded. "But I'm not sure if they will understand me. That's why I'd really appreciate it if you came along."

"I don't know," Miss Martian said. "I really can't read the minds of animals . . . not that I've ever tried."

"Will you at least come with me?" Katana asked. "Please?"

"All right," Miss Martian agreed. "But I can't promise anything."

Usually the Ghost Crabs came to Katana. This time, she went to them.

"This is where they sometimes hang out," Katana told Miss Martian as they entered Harmony Garden. "According to my research, they live underground. But they seem to like it here when the sun's out."

The garden looked the same as before, but with one difference. Katana had enlisted Frost and Supergirl to enhance it. Supergirl had dug a small pool. Frost had filled it with ice, and then Supergirl melted the ice with her heat vision to create a peaceful pond.

A sea of flowers surrounded them, their petals gently rippling in the breeze. Miss Martian paused to inhale the perfume.

Slowly, the Ghost Crabs came out from under leaves and behind bushes. "Hello!" Katana said brightly. "I've brought a friend."

The crabs turned to Miss Martian, who gave them a tiny wave. Some waved their claws back at her.

"I'm not sure how to tell you this," Katana told them, "but Principal Waller would rather you not follow me around everywhere and, for that matter, um . . . disrupt classes anymore."

The Ghost Crabs stood unmoving. Katana turned to Miss Martian. "See, I don't think they understand me. After all, they're crabs, and I don't speak crab. Do you?"

Miss Martian gave her a smirk that said, *Do I look like I speak crab?* "Maybe I can get some impressions of feelings, or something. . . ."

Her eyes grew big. Miss Martian stood very still and stared at the crabs, nodding her head. Then she took in a deep breath, relaxed, and exhaled.

"What is it?" Katana asked.

Miss Martian held up her hand. She chose her words before speaking. "Not only do they understand you," she said, "but they have also sent you a message."

"

CHAPTER 24

■ ■ ■ a message that could affect the world."

Katana's heart was racing. "What? What is it?" she asked. The Ghost Crabs had marshaled themselves in rows of ten again. All were standing at attention. Not a single one moved.

Miss Martian shook her head. "It's *so* weird," she said. "I've never been able to read the mind of a crab before."

"What did they say?" Katana pressed. "Miss Martian, focus!"

Miss Martian bent down to the Ghost Crab leader. She kept nodding. "Okay. Hmmm. Okay," she said before standing back up.

"This is truly amazing," Miss Martian mused. "I don't think anyone in my family has experienced this. Not even my cousin J'Onn, and he is really great at reading minds."

"MISS MARTIAN!" Katana heard herself demand.

When Miss Martian looked taken aback, Katana instantly

regretted losing her temper. "I'm so sorry," she said. "But you said there's a message that could affect the world. What are they saying?"

"Yes, yes," Miss Martian said. "Okay, right, the message. I'm getting a message from all the Ghost Crabs, sort of like chatter. So much that it's hard to understand. But from what I can tell, the main message is that there is danger coming our way. Katana, they want you to know that it is up to you to thwart this. The future is in your hands."

Katana could not believe what she was hearing. Danger was coming to Super Hero High!

"What am I supposed to do?" Katana asked, but when she and Miss Martian looked down, the Ghost Crabs had quietly disappeared again.

"Supers!" Katana called out. "Take your places."

Instantly, the goofing off and gossiping stopped, and like the well-trained super heroes that they were, the teens took their places. Katana had directed the fencing team to gather on the massive Heroball field outside the gym. They needed plenty of room for what she had in mind.

"Fighting stance!" Katana yelled. "And . . . go!"

Paired off, the Super teens looked as though they

were trying to decimate each other. That was far from the case, though. Instead, they were battling each other in an effort to train longer and harder than ever before, to make themselves better. Katana had Arrowette and Cyborg help with swords, and Lady Shiva oversaw the martial arts. With such uncertainty looming, Katana knew that she too would need all the help she could get.

Waller stood by observing and nodding. She pulled Katana aside.

"I like what you are doing," the principal said. "This mash-up of martial arts and swordsmanship. It's important for us to be able to supplement our powers with other methods of fighting. It's an element of surprise that keeps the bad guys on edge. Keep up the good work!"

Just then Batgirl raced up to Waller. "I've been monitoring the airwaves," she said. "My Geographical Scanner is telling me that something off the charts is happening. It's caused a disruption in the ocean's currents and created a tsunami in the Chugoku region of Japan."

Katana felt panic wash over her. That was near her hometown. She hoped her parents were safe.

"Who's causing this?" Waller asked. She lowered her voice. "What can you tell me?"

"I haven't got a strong lock on it yet, but it appears to be a large reptile. The initial indications show that the wave is gaining speed and strength."

"Continue your research," Waller instructed. She turned to Katana. "Can you train these Supers even faster? We may be called in on this, and I want everyone to have every advantage possible."

Katana nodded.

"Well?" Principal Waller bellowed. "What are you standing around for? You all have work to do!"

There was no time to sleep, and hardly any time to eat. Katana was exhausted—as were the rest of the Supers. She was in the Bat-Bunker along with Supergirl.

"Any news?" Katana asked. She handed Batgirl a sandwich.

"It appears to be a dragon," Batgirl said, biting into the peanut butter protein baguette that the cooks made when Supers needed quick fuel. She adjusted the controls on her tech board and a hazy figure appeared on-screen. With her fingers flying over the keyboard, Batgirl was able to zoom in on the creature, cleaning it up digitally so that they could see it. "Thanks to Supergirl, I was able to secure some DNA."

"I flew to Japan to see if I could help, and while I was there, Batgirl called me on our com bracelets," Supergirl said. "I was able to bring back a steel plate from the damaged ship hull that the reptile had recently attacked. Whatever it was had already moved on. I didn't get a visual because I had to save the sailors."

Katana looked at the ship's plate leaning in the corner. There were three long score-marks in the metal, like they had been raked by some creature's horrible talons.

Next, Batgirl scanned the photo into a VaC (Villains and Criminals) program she had created for her father, Police Commissioner Gordon.

"This could take a while," she said while the database ran through thousands of profiles.

"Look!" Supergirl said, pointing to the screen.

"That was fast!" Batgirl noted.

Katana stared at the profile, then read it out loud.

"'Dragon King. Wanted criminal. Cold-blooded. Komodo dragon with powers of strength, flight, and a toxic bite. Armed and extremely dangerous.'"

The trio stared at the screen. Something about him was familiar, Katana thought, but what?

Batgirl began accessing her computer resources. "I'm picking up military and police scanners," she explained. "This 'Dragon King' is moving through small towns and big cities, causing mayhem and destruction along the way. But even worse, it appears that he's amassing an army of handpicked volunteers—mostly criminals—whom he enhances with reptilian genetic material."

"Why? What does he want?" Supergirl asked.

Batgirl pushed her chair away from her control panels. "That, I don't know," she said, shaking her head. "There's not a lot of information on him. He seems to have mostly operated in the shadows."

Katana felt a thud in the pit of her stomach. *Whatever he's after has something to do with me.*

Soon it was all over the news. Lois Lane had broadcast that the Dragon King was indeed headed toward Metropolis. Commissioner Gordon and his police department were on high alert. Waller called a special assembly.

"Students," she said, "this is serious." Parasite stopped sweeping and leaned on his broom, listening. Katana sat between Batgirl and Big Barda. No one moved. "Our sources tell us that there is an enemy who is on the path toward Metropolis, and our intelligence says that his ultimate destination is Super Hero High." Katana squeezed Batgirl's hand. "I will need some of you to fan out and assist those in need as the Dragon King causes destruction in his wake. You will be charged with protecting the citizenry. Others will stay on campus, training and getting ready." She paused before adding, "Supers, you must prepare for battle."

Prepare for battle, Katana thought. Where had she heard that before? Suddenly, a chill ran through her.

> These Samurai swords
> Entrusted to Katana
> The story unfolds.
>
> These Samurai swords
> Entrusted to Katana
> Prepare for battle.

CHAPTER 25

Exhilaration—and even a little panic—ran through Katana as she formulated a plan for what to do next. Though there were stronger and more confident Supers, it was Miss Martian she turned to.

"The haiku hold the key," Katana explained. "They are telling me to prepare for battle, but I need guidance. You said you thought the Ghost Crabs were trying to tell me something. Can we go to them, please? I need all the help I can get!"

"I'll do what I can," Miss Martian answered, "but you know I don't function well under pressure."

Katana nodded. "We'll do what we have to do together."

Miss Martian beamed and for once didn't look like she was going to turn invisible.

The Ghost Crabs were restless. As Katana neared Harmony Garden, they scampered into their ordered ranks.

"Ghost Crabs," Katana said. "I know the Dragon King is headed our way and that there is a battle brewing. But I don't know why. The swords appeared out of nowhere, and then a week later, so did you. And the haiku—what about the haiku? I know it's all connected. If you have a specific message for me, now is the time to share it."

The Ghost Crabs stood still.

"Miss Martian?" Katana said, motioning toward a cluster of trees.

"Hello!" Miss Martian said, addressing the Ghost Crabs as she stepped out of the shadows of the trees and bent down. Her voice was strong but kind. "Please, just focus. I am sensing there is something you'd like Katana to know. But when all of you are thinking at the same time, it's hard for me to figure out what you are trying to say. If there was just one of you, maybe, who could speak for all, that might make it easier."

The Ghost Crabs scattered, forming small groups, and looked like they were in conference. Then they returned to formation. One Ghost Crab scampered forward. It was deep teal-blue and brown, and on its shell the warrior face looked strong and confident.

Miss Martian gently gestured for the Ghost Crab to lift

himself into the air so that they could "talk" eye to eye. Katana watched with awe as the shy alien's face became determined and strong. Finally, the Ghost Crab floated back down and returned to its place in the formation. Miss Martian looked at Katana.

"Dragon King seeks to own the Muteki Sword," she said. Katana's heart fluttered. The Muteki Sword was the sword of legend, also known as the Invincible Sword because whoever possessed it was accorded great powers.

Miss Martian continued. "Dragon King has been quietly seeking the sword for decades. Now he has reason to believe it is at Super Hero High. . . ."

Batgirl was in her Bat-Bunker tracking Dragon King's path. The Supers that Waller had sent out were in search-and-rescue mode. With each city Dragon King crossed, he grew stronger, adding to his own force of fighters, now numbering eighty-three.

"What do you think?" Katana asked Batgirl when she finished relaying Miss Martian's findings.

"It makes perfect sense—why didn't I think of that?" Batgirl replied. "There are one hundred swords and one hundred Ghost Crabs."

"So one sword for each crab?" Katana said. "But the swords are so big and the crabs are so small."

"Maybe they are supposed to guard them," Batgirl ventured.

"But now that the Dragon King has narrowed his search for the swords, the crabs came to Super Hero High for help. And that means the legend of the Muteki Sword is true!" Katana guessed.

"You think it's here?" Wonder Woman asked as she walked in.

"Why else would he amass an army? He wants the sword and is willing to fight to get it," Katana went on.

"Lois Lane just reported that Dragon King and his army of mutant reptiles are headed straight here," Bumblebee said as she buzzed into the room. She made herself full-sized. "We have to be ready, and soon!"

"The haiku said to prepare for battle," Katana noted. "And so we are. I hope it's enough."

"We hardly have a choice," Supergirl said as she joined them. "Look!"

Batgirl had access to every security camera on the planet. She had multiple visuals up on her computer screen. The main one showed a bridge that had almost been destroyed by Dragon King, who was as tall as two men. Super hero twins Thunder and Lightning could be seen charging toward the bridge. Using her powerful shockwaves, Thunder was able to prevent it from falling as the air vibrated and created a safety cushion. Meanwhile, Lightning generated bolts of electrical energy to solder the metal back in place, while other Supers made sure the cars and their passengers were taken to safety.

"It's just as bad as it looks," Lois Lane reported on the news feed now running in the corner of Batgirl's screen. "The only question is, just who is Dragon King and what is he after?"

"The Muteki Sword," Katana whispered. She put her hand on her own sword for comfort.

"But which one is the Muteki?" Supergirl asked.

"That, I don't know. It could be any of them," Katana admitted.

A small voice behind them said, "The sword will reveal itself only to the one whose spirit reflects the highest ideals of a noble warrior."

"Miss Martian," Batgirl said, "did the Ghost Crabs tell you that?"

The Martian girl became visible. She nodded.

"That means someone at Super Hero High could be using the Muteki Sword, bring it to its full potential, and, in doing so, prove that they are worthy," Katana continued. She paused and looked at her friends. "But who?"

CHAPTER 26

"We stand before you with information that will be crucial in the battle you are about to face," Principal Waller said solemnly. Behind her the teachers stood tall, their faces serious. In the back of the auditorium, Parasite listened in.

"Katana, please join me," Waller said.

Katana stepped up to the microphone. "We have received information, thanks to Miss Martian and Batgirl," she said, "that Dragon King will be arriving here soon. He has an army that he has genetically modified with reptilian DNA, most likely granting them enhanced speed and reflexes and who knows what other powers. However, they are merely distractions. What Dragon King is after is the Muteki Sword—one that makes its owner invincible."

There was a stirring in the auditorium. Many had heard rumors of this sort of weapon, but none had ever thought they'd get to see such a wonder.

Beast Boy raised his hand and asked, "Are you saying that one of the swords we're using in fencing could be the Invincible Sword? That one of us could be the true owner of it. That someone—say, me—could hold that power?"

"Supers," Katana said, "you must fight with all of your powers, but also use the sword you have been assigned. We don't know which one holds the power, or which one of you, if any, can ignite it. But what we do know is that Dragon King will be looking to fight each and every person holding a sword, testing out the swords until he finds what he is looking for."

Katana turned to Waller, who said, "Super heroes, retrieve your swords and prepare for battle!"

Never had the students of Super Hero High been so focused. As Katana oversaw them practicing with the swords for one last time, she called out orders. With the Supers gathered outside, swords in hand, Katana noticed the Ghost Crabs looking on from the sidelines, watching as they did during practice. Only, this was real.

"You ready for this?" Katana asked Wonder Woman.

"Always," the Amazon princess responded as she tightened her indestructible bracelets and adjusted her shield.

Katana smiled and turned to watch the others prepare.

"Cheetah, tighten your grip!

"Barda, loosen your grip!

"Raven, use a sweeping gesture!

"Harley, put the video camera down!"

"Aw, but I need to document all of this for Harley's Quinntessentials," Harley cried out. "The world will want to watch!"

Both Katana and Wonder Woman gave her a stern look.

"All right," she grumbled, picking up the sword inlaid with red rubies. "But after we win this thing, I get exclusive interviews!"

Just then, Batgirl walked up to Katana.

"I think the genetic material Dragon King is using comes from Komodo dragons," Batgirl said. "They have bites that are extremely toxic—not to mention claws, teeth, and tough hides. He has his own sword, too, a heavy one with notches in it for each battle he has won. This guy is dangerous, but then I don't have to tell you that."

"Thanks, Batgirl," Katana said, absorbing the information. She called to her co-captains. "Lady Shiva, Cyborg, Arrowette, gather the Supers. I have an announcement!"

Soon, one hundred Super Hero High teens stood at attention with the swords by their sides, waiting to hear what their captain had to say. Katana looked over the fencing team. Just weeks ago they were goofing off with the swords. Today, they were prepared to do battle.

"These swords have been entrusted to you," Katana told them. "They are not yours to keep; however, they are yours to use. One of them may be magical, but that has yet to be seen.

"You each have special powers and skills. I am not asking you to abandon them, but rather, to enhance them with the swords. Together, we will stand ready to face the enemy."

There was a lot of excited and nervous chatter. This was what the Supers had been training for for most of their lives.

Harley turned her camera back on. "Who do you think the great warrior is who will activate the Muteki Sword?" she asked the students nearest her.

Everyone had their own theory.

"I don't know how to say this without sounding like I'm bragging," Beast Boy said. "But I'm pretty sure it's me."

"I think it's probably Supergirl who can ignite the sword," Big Barda said earnestly.

"It could be me," said Star Sapphire. "Or maybe Frost?"

"It could be any one of us," Hawkgirl said.

As everyone called their parents and talked nervously among themselves, Katana set out in search of the Ghost Crabs, who were now nowhere to be found.

"I'd love to have you by my side," she told Miss Martian.

Despite the circumstances, Miss Martian beamed. "Without reading your mind, I knew you'd say that, and I'd like that, too," she replied.

But other than the warm breeze and the blooming flowers, Harmony Garden was empty. Disheartened, Katana sniffed one of the snowballs, and that was when it hit her: she knew where the Ghost Crabs were.

"You were right!" Miss Martian said. "The place where it all started."

It had been a while since Katana had been in the underground aqueduct. She liked the darkness, and the cool was calming, unlike aboveground, where there was managed chaos. The Ghost Crabs were in the tunnel that was now filled with shallow water. Katana knelt down at the water's edge.

"I thought I'd find you back here," she said. "I don't know if you can even understand me. But I am honored that you have entrusted me with the swords. Like you, I will do my best to keep them safe. I don't know who they belong to, but they must be very important for you to have—"

"They belong to the Ghost Crabs," Miss Martian said.

Katana shook her head. "I'm not sure I understand.

The crabs are so small—how could they possibly wield the swords?"

"Not in this life, they can't," Miss Martian said, her eyes closed. She nodded as if finally understanding something. "But in another life, these swords belonged to Samurai. The Ghost Crabs are the spirits of those fallen warriors."

Katana's heart began to race. Suddenly, it all made sense. But what she couldn't understand was why the Ghost Crabs had picked her to protect the swords.

"Katana!" someone cried out.

It was Supergirl.

"There you are! Batgirl says to tell you that Dragon King is less than an hour away."

The Ghost Crabs began to stir.

One by one they exited the water until they were all on land.

"They seek to fight," Miss Martian explained. "Here in the aqueducts, where it is peaceful, they are preparing for battle. Mentally and physically."

Katana looked at them with their warrior faces imprinted on their shells like beautiful paintings.

"No, I'm sorry," she said. "I can't let you do this."

The Ghost Crabs moved forward, but Katana stood still. "I honor you, ancient Samurai," she said, bowing. "But you are spirits of warriors who have fought in battle and are now between two worlds: the ghost world and the real world. Those of us who are of this present world will fight for you. This is a battle for the living to honor those who have passed, and I promise you, we will do our best. You have my word."

Miss Martian, Supergirl, and Katana waited for a reaction. When they got none, Katana began to panic. Dragon King was approaching fast, but she wanted the blessing of the Ghost Crabs. Slowly, the crabs turned around and marched back into the shallow aqueduct.

"We've got to go," Supergirl reminded her. "He's coming."

Katana turned to exit when Miss Martian called out, "Wait! They have a message for you!"

A conch shell was floating on the surface of the water. Katana fished it out and listened to it . . .

> These Samurai swords
> Entrusted to Katana
> Tranquil be the mind.

CHAPTER 27

Final preparations were being made. Mr. Fox was testing everyone's weapons. Wildcat was reminding the students to stretch and flex. Liberty Belle was reciting scenes from great battles in history. Crazy Quilt was checking costumes, making sure they were in fighting form. Doc Magnus was helping Batgirl make sure the school's tech was in working order, and Police Commissioner Gordon was in Metropolis marshaling the city's police force.

> *These Samurai swords*
> *Entrusted to Katana*
> *Tranquil be the mind.*

Katana repeated the haiku over and over again. What did it mean? How could anyone be tranquil when faced with an approaching reptile army? Her mind was racing and her body electric in anticipation of what lay ahead.

There was nothing left to do but wait.

Batgirl was in her Bat-Bunker squinting at an interactive map on one of her computers. Wonder Woman and Supergirl looked over her shoulder as Katana rushed in. Most of the Supers had requested that they be allowed to keep working out with the swords, so Katana had left Arrowette, Cyborg, and Lady Shiva in charge.

"I'm going to need all of you with me," Katana said. She tried to focus, but she was still thinking about the mysterious haiku. What had the conch shell meant by being tranquil?

"ETA in fourteen minutes," Batgirl announced. "Either here in the bunker or out in the midst of the battle, I'm with you," she assured her, adding, "ETA means 'estimated time of arrival.' Dragon King and his army will be here in fourteen minutes— Oops. Make that thirteen."

Nearby, Wonder Woman's expression turned warrior fierce.

Katana looked serious. "Okay, Supers, time to go!" she said.

Outside, the sky had darkened.

"It's the same sky," Hawkgirl whispered to Katana.

"What do you mean?" Katana asked.

"The day we rescued Parasite, the sky looked like this

right before the ocean began churning and destroyed his raft."

Katana nodded. Hawkgirl was right.

"Supers, prepare for battle!" Wonder Woman called as she raised her shield toward the sky. She stepped back, and Katana took her place.

"Remember what I told you in training. The swords are a supplement to your weapons and powers, not a replacement. Dragon King is looking for a particular sword, one that legend says will grant the wielder invincible powers. I don't know if that is true or just ancient lore, but I do know that Dragon King will not stop until he finds it. When the sword is discovered, we will rally around the one in possession of it," Katana promised. "Though it is a single sword he wants to claim, we are and will always be a team. We will fight together and defend each other!"

Her friends and fellow students roared in response. They were ready to defend their school, the world, and each other.

As the noise died down, the dark-gray clouds grew thicker as they blocked the sun. Churning above like waves in the ocean, they sank lower and lower until they almost touched the amethyst that topped Super Hero High's tower. Then it was as if the gem punctured the clouds, and they broke with a blast so loud that windows shattered, sending shards of glass raining down.

Where the sky had sliced open, Dragon King descended, followed by his army—some flying on leathery wings, others marching on foot from all sides of the school. Katana observed her enemy. He was big and muscled. He wore armor even though his thick scales would have been protection enough. His sharp teeth looked chiseled and deathly sharp, and his eyes were small but bright, reflecting the evil within him. Dragon King's tail was capable of knocking out any number of warriors with one swipe, and in his clawed hand was a sword of his own.

Katana had never seen a bigger or more powerful-looking sword. As Dragon King swung the sharp, thick blade over his head, the sound of air being sliced echoed throughout the school. Some Supers backed away even though he was not near them. Others stepped forward. Katana remained rooted, observing, thinking, planning.

Dragon King surveyed the landscape, summing up the Supers and his own army, who stood at ragged attention. A wicked smile crossed his face as he opened his massive mouth and roared. Fire spewed from him as he reduced Harmony Garden to scorched twigs and branches. Pleased with himself, Dragon King knocked over the statue of Justice—the school's symbolic muse—and leapt nimbly onto the stone pedestal and looked around the school.

"Nice place you have here," he said to Principal Waller, who stood out in front of her students.

She remained still, with her arms crossed and her jaw set. Her glare was so cold it gave Katana the chills.

"Well, look at all these students," Dragon King said as his army gathered. "Reminds me of when I went to a school like this. But of course, mine was not as elite or as nice as this one. Oh, how I hated school," he said, making hissing *tsk-tsk* sounds. "I was very unpopular and had only one friend. But look at me now! Here I am at Super Hero High and everyone wants to get to know me. How about that?"

Katana noted that she had never seen anything like him before. Or had she? There was something unsettlingly familiar about Dragon King.

"You!" he shouted.

Katana looked around. He was talking to her?

"Do you like it at this school?"

"Yes," Katana said in a clear, strong voice.

Dragon King let out a deep, long laugh and brandished his sword. "Well, let's see if we can change that."

PART THREE

CHAPTER 28

"**A**rmy, attack!" Dragon King roared so loud the ground shook. He stayed on the pedestal as his army raced into battle.

Katana flashed a look at Wonder Woman.

"Supers, ready . . . go!" Wonder Woman yelled as she flew above them, leading the first wave of Supers.

There was no time for Katana to be scared. She had fought in battles before, including the one against Granny Goodness's army of Female Furies. Katana looked over at Big Barda, who had once helped rule the Furies and had fought the Supers. Now she was on their side, and Katana couldn't help but smile at the way Barda shone in battle.

Big Barda held her Mega Rod in one hand and one of the Japanese swords sheathed on her side, ready to use it when the time was right. As a mutant reptilian soldier raced toward her, Barda lifted her Mega Rod high and swung it—

boom!—sending the reptile flying across the school grounds.

"One down, dozens to go!" Barda said, looking pleased. "But who's counting?"

"Behind you!" shouted Bumblebee, who was flying after a winged warrior headed straight toward Barda.

Big Barda twirled around, unsheathing the sword, and swung it, striking the armored enemy with such force that his shield cracked and he flew backward. The human-reptile hybrid didn't stop until he hit the administration building.

Barda looked at the sword, now bent out of shape. Using her incredible strength, she straightened it until it was as good as new.

"Well, that's not the Muteki Sword," Dragon King said, yawning as he gazed out over the battle.

Katana realized his strategy. He was going to let his mutants fight his war, and if and when he saw a Super whose sword was indestructible or gave some sign of bestowing great power to its wielder, then he would attack. As she looked at him, Katana felt a connection, albeit an unsettling one. However, there was no time to ruminate.

"I need backup!" someone called.

In an instant, Katana was fighting alongside Cheetah, who was battling a trio of reptilians. "Three to one? Not fair," Cheetah purred. "But three to two? That's just about right!"

Katana and Cheetah easily defeated their opponents with

a series of high kicks and low punches executed in tandem.

Near the vehicle building, Batgirl was up against a hulking mutant reptile who had uprooted a tree trunk and was now swinging it at her, causing dirt from the roots to fly everywhere.

"Seriously?" Batgirl said. "Poison Ivy is not going to be happy about that."

Batgirl pulled a small canister from her Utility Belt and unleashed its gaseous contents in the snarling mutant's face. After taking a deep breath of the gas, the lizard warrior dropped the tree and fell to its knees. Batgirl bonked it over the head with the handle of her sword, knocking it out. "Well, that was easy," she said. "I *knew* I should have made more reptile repellent after it worked so well on Croc."

As the Supers continued to fight, Katana joined in battles and had a few of her own. No one was a match for the granddaughter of a Samurai super hero, and several of Dragon King's warriors fled at the sight of her.

Fighting at Katana's side, Supergirl said, "He's a mutterer."

"Who?" Katana asked. She backflipped over a pair of reptiles who were about to attack Thunder and Lightning.

"Dragon King," Supergirl said as she tossed a couple of surly mutants into the air and watched Frost freeze them before they fell. "I'm using my super-hearing."

"What's he saying?" Katana asked. She looked around, proud of what she saw. Beast Boy had turned into a reptile himself, confusing the enemy. Arrowette was hurling arrows, some flaming, faster than the enemy could take in what was happening. Wonder Woman had several tied up in her Lasso of Truth, and all were crying and saying that Dragon King had tricked them.

"He's not impressed with any of the swords he sees," Supergirl reported, "though Dragon King is impressed with us."

"As he should be," Katana noted. She motioned to Hawkgirl and Bumblebee.

Both were flying circles around the enemy, and while Hawkgirl rounded them up, Bumblebee was blasting electric stings and bringing them to their misshapen hands and knees.

Over in her student project garden, the usually sweet Poison Ivy was yelling at the reptile warriors. "Do. NOT. Trample. My. PLANTS!!!" she warned. When they didn't listen, Poison Ivy reached into her bag for the flower bombs she had created in Mr. Fox's class. She lobbed the weapons at them and watched with glee as they exploded, creating a net of thorny rose vines that captured several enemies at once.

Supergirl and Katana high-fived each other. Before they

could say anything, they were suddenly surrounded by a dozen angry mutants. The girls smiled at one another.

"This is going to be fun!" Supergirl said.

"*Going to be?* I thought it already was!" Katana replied. "Three, two, one . . . let's go!"

As Supergirl charged the warriors, Katana rolled into a trio of them, sending them flying into the air. Then, using her martial arts skills, she disarmed them while doing multiple kicks to bring them down. Taking out her sword, she fought six more with ease. Calling on the moves Onna had taught her, Katana displayed expert skill and grace. Though it was a battle, it looked more like a ballet—except, of course, when her enemies fell one by one, yelling "Oompf!" and "Ugh!" and "I give up!"

With the dozen captured, it took less than a second for them to be tied up by The Flash, who ran around them with handcuffs and steel ropes in hand. Katana smiled at Supergirl, who, instead of smiling back, looked stricken.

"What's the matter?" Katana asked.

"*He's* what's the matter."

Katana was surprised to find Miss Martian standing next to Supergirl.

"You tell her," Supergirl said. "I could only hear his muttering, but you may know more."

Miss Martian gulped and her voice trembled. "Katana,

Dragon King wasn't impressed with any of the Supers using their swords . . . until he saw *you!*"

"Army!" Dragon King roared. "Keep fighting, but give me space. There is one battle I want to fight for myself. One that is long overdue!"

Katana turned to see Dragon King, a sinister smile on his face, rising off the pedestal and flying toward her. Miss Martian disappeared. Supergirl balled up her fists and rose into the air to greet him.

"No," Katana said sharply. "No," she said again, softer this time. "I will fight him myself."

"You sure?" Supergirl asked, looking uncertain.

"Assist the others," she said. "I got this."

As Supergirl flew away, Dragon King landed in front of Katana, casting a shadow over her.

"Why, hello, little lady. You must be the granddaughter of Onna-bugeisha Yamashiro," he said. His voice was smooth and untrustworthy. "I have heard of you."

"That's funny," Katana said as they slowly circled each other. "I'd never heard of you before today."

"No?" Dragon King hissed, looking insulted. "Your grandmother never ssspoke of me? She told me all about you and how even though you were young, you already were showing signs of one day being a Samurai super hero."

Katana was surprised. Onna had spoken to him about her? *Wait!*

Suddenly, it made sense. Dragon. Dragon King. Dragon Prince. They were one and the same. Katana flashed back to the teak chest in her room. There were photos—photos of Onna with Dragon Prince. She had even talked about him in her diary. But he was scrawny back then. So, he had changed himself, Katana noted, *and* given himself a promotion!

"You were friends?" Katana asked, surprised.

"She was my friend," he said, laughing. "In the end, I was not hersss."

CHAPTER 29

Katana stood very still, waiting for Dragon King to continue. He licked his crusty lips with his lizard tongue and smiled his serpentine smile. "She had something I wanted," he said, looking at the battles that were taking place all around him. "We agreed to meet, years after high school. . . ."

That was when the truth hit Katana. It struck her so hard, she gasped and held her stomach. Her parents had said that on the night Onna had perished, she was to meet up with an old friend from high school. Of course it had to have been him. She had trusted him, and he betrayed her.

Dragon King laughed, though nothing was funny. "Yesss, yesss," he hissed. "I think you know who I am now. I wanted the Muteki Sword, the one your grandmother had. But the sword I took from her didn't hold any special powers. So I . . . Well, we all know how this ssstory ended."

Katana was speechless.

"But you, my dear, you're pretty good with the sword, and your style reminds me of your grandmother's—fluid. So then, while the others battle in search of the Invincible Sword, I suggest we have a little fight of our own. Once I get rid of you, I can focusss on my mission. What do you sssay to that? I can't have Onna-bugeisha Yamashiro's little granddaughter standing in my way, can I?"

A chill ran through Katana. In her nightmare, she was running, running. Something or someone was chasing her. Now she knew who it was. It was Dragon King. Katana's nightmare had turned real.

"I'm not afraid of you," Katana announced, standing tall. Grief mixed with rage had unnerved her, but she couldn't let Dragon King know that she harbored any fear.

"Tsssk, tsssk. Oh, Katana, you're just like Onna-bugeisha," Dragon King said, shaking his head in mock sadness. Though he looked nothing like his high school self, the eyes, the beady eyes, were the same. Back then he had looked weak, but the villain before her now looked supremely strong and confident.

Dragon King sharpened the blade of his sword against the metal-like scales on his leg. "She was fearless, yesss, but she had her flaws," he mused. "The great ones always do, you know. Are you one of the great ones, Katana? Is that your goal? I wonder what your fatal flaw will be?"

He was just trying to rattle her, Katana reminded herself. "My grandmother had no flaws," she said defiantly. As much as she ached to attack him and avenge her grandmother's death, she knew that Dragon King knew about young Onna, and had stories she longed to hear. "Tell me about her."

"Say pleassse," Dragon King said, condescension mixing with his breathy reptilian hiss. He was enjoying her discomfort. Katana gritted her teeth and glared at him. The reptile man chuckled. "Well, close enough."

"Let's sssee now," he said slowly. "Onna was very popular in school. I'll bet you are, too, aren't you?" When Katana did not answer, his eyes narrowed. "I hate popular—it's overrated. Those who are popular have it easy. Look at me. I wasn't popular. I didn't look like this." He flexed his massive muscles, and then with a roar, flames blasted from his mouth as he set Crazy Quilt's quirky vintage sports car on fire. Crazy Quilt's gasped sob was heard above the roar of battle.

"That's all about you. What can you tell me about my grandmother?" Katana asked. She was using as much restraint as she could muster.

"Ah, yesss," he said, looking off into the distance. Frost was now covering the car in sheets of ice to put out the flames. Mutants were fighting Supers, and it looked like the Supers were winning. Commissioner Gordon had rows of specially reinforced armored transport vehicles from Metropolis's

S.C.U., and he was rounding up Dragon King's soldiers and hauling them away.

Still, Dragon King acted like he couldn't be bothered with all that. "Yesss, Onna-bugeisha Yamashiro was a mighty Samurai. Beloved by all—well, mossst. Her fatal flaw?" He smiled at Katana, showing his lethal lizard tongue. "Onna's fatal flaw was that she trusted me."

Every part of Katana's body tensed. She longed to lunge at him but practiced restraint. The truth was what she was after.

"I told her that I wanted to sssee her," Dragon King continued. "That I had a present for her after all these years. She foolishly agreed to meet me. But it wasn't me who had something for her. She had sssomething I wanted."

He stopped to savor the words and let his eyes linger over the sword in Katana's hand, and continued, "The Muteki Sword, the legendary Invincible Sword. Everyone knew there was a famous female Samurai super hero, but no one knew who it was. I knew, though. It could have been no one else. With her swordplay, her strength and determination—and her quaint habit of wanting to sssave people from evil—why, obviously, it had to be my old ssschoolmate Onna-bugeisha. And how did she do it? With the aid of the sword, of course."

Katana could hardly breathe, but it wasn't because of the smoke from the now-smoldering car. "Please, continue," she said, unsure if she really wanted to hear what he had to say next. Her hands were sweaty, and it was hard to grip her sword.

Dragon King wrapped his claws around his own sword and began to circle her. In turn, Katana pivoted. They moved around and around each other as slowly and surely as the moon around the Earth and the Earth around the sun. And equally unable to escape one another.

"We met by the ocean," he continued. "There were massive dunes, and the wind blew sand in my face. I told Onna that I wanted her sssword, and when she asssked me why, I said, 'To rule the world, of course.'" Dragon King shook his head. "I was honessst. She didn't like that.

"So we battled. It may not have been fair that I had one hundred accomplices to help me, but I do what needs to be done. In the end, I did get her sword. But she double-crosssed me! It was not the Muteki Sword at all!" he roared. "She didn't have it!" His eyes narrowed as he looked over his army fighting the Supers with swords.

Bumblebee was in top form, her wings carrying her as she flew headfirst toward a mutant and zapped him with an electric blast.

Wonder Woman had a sword in one hand and her Lasso of Truth in the other.

Cyborg was fighting alongside Lady Shiva, who was

combining lethal martial arts moves with sword fighting.

And Harley Quinn had somehow mounted a camera to her sword, fighting with such glee that her crazy laugh was enough to make the mutants flee from her even before she could engage them in battle. "Come back!" she yelled as she chased them around the school. "I want to get you on video!"

Dragon King waved a dismissive hand at the commotion. "One of those swords left in play is the legendary Muteki. I have ssspent the last decade of my life trying to find it, and will not ssstop until I do!"

"How do you know it's one of them?" Katana asked.

He shook his head as if she had asked him a stupid question. "If Onna didn't have the sword, it was a given that another Samurai must have had it."

The two continued circling one another, each waiting for the other to draw their sword first. With each step, the circle grew smaller as they got closer and closer to each other. So close that Katana could feel his hot breath.

"And so you are here," Katana said. Her normally bright eyes darkened. "Now what?"

CHAPTER 30

"**O**h, Katana. You are so insssightful," Dragon King said sarcastically. "Yes, here I am now. Legend has it that there are one hundred mighty Samurai swords from fallen warriors, all enshrined in an underwater temple."

"Go on." Katana baited him as she steeled herself for battle. She thought about Onna and how she had trusted Dragon Prince. Katana did not feel the same way.

"Finally, I found the Temple of the Sssacred Swords," he bragged. "But the swords were gone! It took a while, but I discovered that they were at Sssuper Hero High, and now I am here to claim what is rightfully mine."

"Rightfully yours?" Katana replied, her anger growing. "Why is it yours? You are not worthy!"

"You speck of a girl!" Dragon King said, spitting. "You bore me. I have no use for you. Out of my way! I need to get to my Muteki, and you are wasssting my valuable time!"

The two drew their swords at the exact same moment.

The clanging of the metal blades echoed across the courtyard. Such was their skill that all the other battles slowed to a stop so that everyone could watch Katana versus Dragon King.

Though he was incredibly strong, she was fast, ducking, leaping, and tumbling so quickly that he had trouble seeing her.

"I'll do away with you and find the Invincible Sword. Then the world will be mine!" Dragon King promised as he towered over her.

"Not if I conquer you first," Katana yelled back.

"I was wrong," he said as their swords struck each other's with such speed and strength that sparks flew. "You aren't as good as your grandmother!"

Her grandmother. For a split second, Katana thought about her beloved Onna, and that was all it took for Dragon King to gain the edge.

"Ha!" he cried as he knocked Katana's sword from her hand. "This is what happened to her, too! All I had to do was mention that I would send my comrades to get her precious Katana—and Onna became distracted!"

He had threatened Onna, saying he would harm her? Katana could not bear the thought of this. As she stood still, she glanced at her sword on the ground. Dragon King inched toward it, dragging his heavy tail. He picked it up.

"It's not very impressive, is it?" he said disdainfully. "You would think that the granddaughter of the world's first female Samurai super hero would have sssomething better than this sssliver of a sword." He swung it in the air. "Not bad. But it's so plain, so light. Not a mighty sword like mine, and nothing like the Muteki, I am sure."

Katana watched in horror as he tossed it aside. It landed near a . . . Ghost Crab? What was it doing there? Katana had told them all to remain underground.

"What is that?" Dragon King said, looking amused. "A little crab scampering away in fear? How quaint."

The crab fearlessly faced the mighty dragon, doing a little hop before it began running circles around him.

"I could use a snack," Dragon King said.

Suddenly, the tiny crab had turned into a green dragon.

"Beast Boy?" Katana whispered, though she could not help but be amused.

"That's right, mama. And I will fight fire with fire," Beast Boy declared, attempting to send flames at Dragon King. When none came out, Dragon King laughed. "Fire with fire," Beast Boy declared again. He took a deep breath, but instead of flames, Beast Boy let out a long, loud burp before turning back into a teen. "Oops," he said, patting his stomach. "My lunch."

"Enough of this playtime," Dragon King yelled, looking disgusted. "I shall have *you* for my lunch!"

He grabbed a surprised Beast Boy and was about to attack him with his horrible bite when Dragon King froze. He began to shake, as if being drained of his powers. He dropped Beast Boy, and only then did Katana see the school janitor gripping Dragon King's tail.

"Parasite, run!" Beast Boy yelled as he scrambled away.

Katana looked over at Parasite, who was focused on Dragon King with an intensity she had never seen from him before. "Soooo much . . . power . . . ," Parasite screamed, refusing to let go. The tighter he held on, the more satisfied Parasite became as he absorbed Dragon King's power, weakening his adversary.

"Get your sword," Parasite finally gasped. "Save yourself. . . ."

Before Katana could react, his eyes closed and, as if suddenly overcome in a blissful coma, Parasite fell motionless to the ground.

CHAPTER 31

Adrenaline surged through Katana's body. Without taking her eyes off her nemesis, she reached for her sword, the one Onna had given her when she was a child. Could it even stand a chance against the Dragon King? She would find out soon enough.

As Katana scrambled to take her fighting stance, Dragon King rose, weakened, angry, and shaken. Though Parasite had somehow drained him of his powers long enough to save Beast Boy, it didn't last long.

"I'm not afraid of you," Katana said. She hoped Dragon King could not hear her heart racing.

He wiped his mouth and snarled. His claws were long and sharp. "Forget the snack, I shall proceed to the main courssse," he said menacingly. She could see him gaining power with each step.

As their swords crashed, Katana fought as hard as she

could. But with each swing, each strike, each roar from the Dragon King, she could feel his strength returning. She was fast, but so was he. And with his enhanced size, Katana knew that she would have to come up with a new strategy to defeat him. With all this happening so fast, she began to lose focus.

Out of the corner of her eye, Katana thought she saw a Ghost Crab. Then more. Two, three, four, they kept coming, and each one was sending her the same message at the same time, until it became more and more clear, louder and louder, like a chant.

> *These Samurai swords*
> *Entrusted to Katana*
> *Tranquil be the mind.*

"Tranquil be the mind," Katana repeated over and over again. "Tranquil be the mind."

For a brief moment, time stood still and Katana was a small girl again, holding the sword her grandmother had given her . . .

"Tatsu," Onna said. "Someday you will be big and strong enough to make this sword your partner. And when you do, remember, you are a team. Your sword will lead you, as you lead it. Go slow. Do not act in haste. Be at one with your weapon. Tranquility rules chaos."

Katana turned to face Dragon King, who was smiling at her, his white teeth bared.

"Tranquility," Katana whispered to herself.

When she shut her eyes, Katana could hear Dragon King laughing. "Oh, little one," he said mockingly as if speaking to a child. "Just because you close your eyes doesn't mean I am gone."

Katana's eyes fluttered open. A look of determination settled on her face. She crouched low with one leg out, then executed a masterful leap, landing silently on the ground near him. She raised her sword high in the air. But instead of swinging wildly like before, Katana did the opposite. She slowed down.

Now circling Dragon King, when the moment was right, Katana seized it—lunging at him, fighting sword against sword with such power that it looked like a firestorm.

Katana did not let her enemy's roars of anger and frustration sway her. She focused on simplifying her fight. Not a breath or movement or motion was wasted. It was as if the sword was leading her, or was it the other way around? This plain sword of hers, which she had owned most of her life, was acting as if it had a life of its own. In her hands, like never before, it wasn't just a sword—it was an extension of her and all her goals and dreams. Katana wasn't just fighting for herself, she was fighting for anyone and everyone her enemy had ever harmed or would harm if he got past her.

Dragon King raised his heavy sword high above his head, but Katana stood her ground. She braced herself, and when his weapon came down to crush her, Katana's sword cut through the air. With a clash of metal so loud that buildings shook, Katana knocked Dragon King's sword from his mighty grip.

His sword flew high and far, and before it landed, Katana did a flying sidekick, knocking the mighty Dragon King to the ground. Katana raised her sword in the air as if to slay the evil dragon. In that moment, for a brief second, her costume seemed to turn into that of a regal Samurai soldier, one with a snowball flower gracing the helmet.

"Onna-bugeisha?" Dragon King said, his voice full of fear and surprise. "You live?"

The mighty Dragon King began to shudder.

"Spare me!" he begged. "Onna, my friend, ssspare me!"

Katana took a deep breath. The Dragon King blinked in disbelief . . . and he would have sworn Onna-bugeisha Yamashiro's armor turned back into Katana's normal super hero costume. Then she stated in a voice that was clear and proud, "I am Katana, formerly Tatsu Yamashiro, granddaughter of Onna-bugeisha Yamashiro, the first female Samurai super hero. I will avenge the harm you have done to my grandmother and countless others!"

"Mercy, please have mercy," Dragon King begged. "Noble granddaughter of Onna-bugeisha Yamashiro, I beg of you, please show me mercy!"

"Like the mercy you showed my grandmother?" Katana asked, her eyes flashing. Then suddenly the haiku began to roll through her mind like a gentle wind.

These Samurai swords
Entrusted to Katana
The story unfolds.

These Samurai swords
Entrusted to Katana
Prepare for battle.

These Samurai swords
Entrusted to Katana
Tranquil be the mind.

Katana looked around. All eyes were on her. Her friends and fellow Supers, her teachers, Principal Waller.

Tranquil be the mind.

As Katana swung her sword, she could hear her enemy cry out. But instead of her sword doing away with Dragon King, the blade merely nicked him. Then, like a punctured tire, he deflated, from a massive beast once bent on destruction to a tiny lizard. Whatever had powered the Dragon King and his mutants dissipated. His army shriveled into small lizards, too. From their hiding places, the Ghost Crabs appeared, chasing away Dragon King and what was left of his army.

Katana breathed in deeply and then exhaled with relief. That was, until she heard someone moan. It was Parasite.

As Wonder Woman led a team to attend to injured Supers, Poison Ivy got to Parasite first, quickly followed by Beast Boy and Supergirl.

"Is he going to be okay?" Supergirl asked.

"This is all my fault," Beast Boy lamented.

"Give her space," Katana said to everyone.

Ivy knelt down beside Parasite. His skin was ashen. Bumblebee flew over with a wicker basket filled with flowers and herbs.

"Breathe in," Poison Ivy said, waving a clutch of scientifically altered herbs under his nose.

Bumblebee took his pulse.

At last Parasite began to stir and Katana could exhale once again. Hawkgirl lifted him up and flew him to Metropolis General Hospital's emergency room, and some of the Supers followed, flanking her. However, Katana remained, knowing he was in good hands.

She stood on the spot where she had defeated Dragon King. Mixed emotions ran through her. It was only then that she noticed the Ghost Crabs had returned. They were lined up in neat rows in front of her, one hundred strong.

Katana smiled at her small friends, but she could not have prepared for what happened next.

CHAPTER 32

One by one, the Ghost Crabs transformed into ethereal versions of the human Samurai warriors they had once been. Strong and noble, they bowed to Katana, their living leader, who had led an army of Supers to fight a battle on their behalf.

One stepped forward. "We are indebted to you," he said. Though strong and handsome, his face looked tired. "The Heikegani legend is the truth. As Ghost Crabs, we are the reincarnation of honored Samurai who have been slain in battle. No longer seeking to avenge, all we ask for in our next lives is peace and tranquility. And we want the reassurance that our swords, which served us admirably, are safe from evil and harm. They are, indeed, a part of us and represent who we were and how we will be remembered."

Katana was speechless.

"Thank you, Katana," he continued, "for protecting the

swords as only the granddaughter of a Samurai super hero could. We knew that we could place our trust in you."

Still unable to speak, she nodded.

"Now, if we could be so humble as to ask one more favor of you?" the Samurai soldier asked.

Katana nodded again.

"It would be an honor to us if you would please accompany the swords back to the Temple of the Sacred Swords under the sea, where they shall reside in peace for all eternity. Can you, will you?"

"Yes," Katana promised. "I can and I shall."

"We are forever in your debt," the Samurai said, stepping back to join the others. Then, in unison, the Samurai warriors bowed once more to the granddaughter of Onna-bugeisha Yamashiro.

As Katana and the rest of the students and staff of Super Hero High looked on, one by one the phantom Samurai warriors turned back into Ghost Crabs.

"They are anxious to return to the calm of the afterlife," Miss Martian said as she appeared by Katana's side.

"After all their battles, they deserve peace," Katana said. "I will make sure their swords are protected from the likes of

Dragon King." She looked around at her friends. "Who will help me get the swords safely to the Temple of the Sacred Swords and fortify it?"

Instantly, everyone raised their hands.

"Come on, Ghost Crabs," Bumblebee said, "I'll take you back to the aqueduct."

"And I'll turn into a swordfish to accompany you back to the temple!" Beast Boy volunteered, adding, "Swordfish. Sword. Fish. Get it? Swordfish!"

Wonder Woman laughed. "I'll fly as you journey under the sea to protect you from any harm that may come from above!"

And so it went, with each Super telling the Ghost Crabs how they would help.

"We have to wait for the waters to return," Batgirl noted. "Then the crabs can return to the ocean the way they arrived."

Batgirl set about mapping out the best route to get to the temple. Using her B.A.T. sonar satellite hookup, she was able to home in on the underwater location of the hidden temple.

Meanwhile, everyone gathered the swords in one spot. Those that were battered were bent back into shape by Wonder Woman, or soldered by Supergirl's heat vision, or hammered by Harley with her mallet. Any jewels that were missing were replaced by Star Sapphire, who used her own personal cache of gems.

"This is going to make a dynamite video special!" Harley said as she worked an ancient sword back into shape. "Hey, Mr. Ghost Crab, mind if I interview you, or what about you there?" But the crabs were too fast for even Harley Quinn. Besides, they had someplace else they'd rather be.

"The water has returned," Parasite reported, already back from the hospital.

Poison Ivy ran up to him and handed him a bouquet of flowers. He pushed them away, but Katana noticed he was hiding a smile—until he remembered he was supposed to be grumpy.

"The water has returned!" Katana said, echoing Parasite. She knew what this meant. "Beast Boy, rally the Ghost Crabs. It's time!"

Beast Boy offered her an impish grin, but got uncharacteristically serious when he saw the injured janitor. "Thank you, sir," he said.

"For what?" Parasite said. He took another deep breath from the colorful bouquet that Poison Ivy had infused with healing scents.

"For saving my life," Beast Boy said. He looked like he was going to cry. When he stepped forward to hug Parasite, the janitor stepped back.

"Sure, kid. You're welcome. But this is probably the last time you'll see me. If anyone asks, you tell 'em that Parasite wasn't so bad after all."

"Sure thing," Beast Boy said, looking confused.

"Where are you going?" Katana asked. "Why won't we see you?"

"Are you going on vacation?" asked Poison Ivy.

"Vacation?" Parasite scoffed. "That's a good one. Noooo, I'll be headed back to prison, most likely. Part of the condition of my parole was that I was never to use my power—the power to drain others of theirs."

"But you did it to save me!" Beast Boy protested.

"Yeah," Parasite muttered. "But the rules are the rules. You know how the Wall can be."

To ensure the swords would make it back safely, the Supers each accompanied and guarded the sword they fought with. That meant some would fly, others would run, and still others would teleport—but no matter how they did it, all would convene at the same destination.

Meanwhile, Beast Boy's green swordfish would lead the Ghost Crabs away from Super Hero High to the temple so they could be sure their swords were safe before continuing on their journey to peace and tranquility.

While her friends and schoolmates prepared for their trip to the other side of the world, Katana went over to the ground where Dragon King had fallen. There were still signs of battle everywhere—but the day seemed crisp and new and the world felt safe again.

Sensing a presence, Katana turned around. There was no one there. "Miss Martian?" she said. "Is that you?"

When there was no answer, Katana looked down to find a Ghost Crab standing alone. The mask that marked the shell looked familiar. "They're all leaving now," she said. "You'd better hurry so you can catch up with them! I will join you soon."

"Katana," she heard a familiar voice say. "Tatsu."

CHAPTER 33

Katana watched as the tiny Ghost Crab changed in front of her eyes. There standing before her was the most regal, glowing Samurai warrior she had ever seen.

"Grandmother!" she cried. Her heart was so full she thought it would burst. "Onna . . ."

"Dear Katana, my love," her grandmother said. Katana heard the familiar gentle melody in her voice. Onna was wearing the Samurai uniform that Dragon King had seen on Katana the moment she had defeated him. The snowball flower was as fresh as if it had just been plucked from Harmony Garden.

Katana was surprised that she was taller than Onna, until she remembered that she had not seen her grandmother since she was a child. Onna smiled warmly at her. "Take your sword," she told her granddaughter.

When she did as she was told, Katana's eyes grew big as

her sword began to glow. "How? Is this . . . ?"

"Yes," Onna said, nodding. "My dearest granddaughter, you have been in possession of the Muteki Sword all this time. Only a true Samurai super hero can wield this invincible weapon. In the hands of anyone else, it is just a sword like any other. When you faced Dragon King, you proved yourself worthy. Revenge is easy, but to pardon an enemy takes even more courage."

When Onna-bugeisha Yamashiro bowed to her, Katana felt her spirit fill with pride and joy . . . and most of all, love.

"Oh, Onna," she wept. "How I've missed you."

Her grandmother held up her hand and whispered something in her ear. Just as Katana was about to ask her what that meant, Onna turned back into a Ghost Crab and, in an instant, was gone.

CHAPTER 34

Beast Boy's swordfish went by sea, and, protected from above by Supergirl and Wonder Woman, the Ghost Crabs rode the ocean currents toward Japan. True to their word, the Supers accompanied the Ghost Crabs' one hundred swords to the Temple of the Sacred Swords. But it was the 101st Super who was in the lead—Katana, the Samurai super hero granddaughter of the legendary Onna-bugeisha Yamashiro. In her hand she carried her own sword, the Muteki Sword.

"We are here to announce the Hero of the Month," Principal Waller said from the stage. The auditorium was packed with Supers. In the back of the room, Parasite gripped his broom.

Katana sat between Harley Quinn and Batgirl. Though it had been a week since she had bid the Ghost Crabs goodbye, they still weighed heavily on her mind, especially one in particular.

"Katana!" Waller boomed as Harley instantly turned her camera on her. "Super Hero High's Super Hero of the Month!"

Cheers filled the room as Beast Boy led the "Ka-tan-a, Ka-tan-a" chant.

Liberty Belle motioned to Katana from where the faculty sat onstage. Her teacher whispered, "Your Legacy project? A-plus! This battle is one for the history books!"

Humbled, Katana looked over the sea of expectant faces before her. She had seen her friends Wonder Woman, Supergirl, and Batgirl receive this honor, but never dreamt that it would be hers one day.

"Katana, we are in your debt," Waller said, her deep voice filling the auditorium. "You had the strength and insight to defeat a known villain, one who had wreaked havoc on so many. And by teaching your fellow Supers the art of the sword and martial arts, you enhanced their already formidable skills. Please, say a few words. . . ."

Katana stepped up to the mike. When she opened her mouth to speak, nothing came out. Public speaking was almost as scary as battle, she thought! Her mind was racing. Then she closed her eyes and breathed. *Tranquil.*

When her eyelids fluttered open, Katana saw her friends

staring at her. "I am humbled by this honor," she began, nodding to Principal Waller. Her voice faltered with emotion as she went on. "I dedicate this award to heroes and Samurai, super or not—and to anyone who has ever found themselves in harm's way while battling evil, saving lives, and making the world a better place."

As she spoke, Katana's voice rose, gaining strength. "A wise woman recently told me," she said, "that when warriors thought they were in possession of the Invincible Sword, they fought harder, better, stronger—trying to live up to its potential." She smiled at her friends. "That is what I saw when I observed you all in battle against Dragon King and his army. You, my fellow Supers, each tried to live up to the potential of the Muteki, when really that potential has been in you all along." Everyone sat up straighter. "The swords didn't make you stronger—you made the swords stronger."

There was a silence as everyone let this sink in. Katana's fingers lightly touched the handle of her sword. Then she began clapping for her friends. Katana was joined by the teachers, who gave their students a standing ovation, and soon everyone was cheering.

Katana waved for them to stop. She pushed the microphone aside, not needing it anymore. "There are two people I would like to share this honor with . . . Miss Martian, please join me on the stage." Though she could not see her,

Katana could feel her presence. "All of you stretched your limits and went beyond your given strengths and powers during this adventure, especially Miss Martian. It is because of her that we were able to communicate with the Ghost Crabs and bring down Dragon King!"

Cheers erupted again as Miss Martian became visible. She was beaming . . . and blushing.

"And Parasite," Katana continued, "who risked his life to save Beast Boy and me, and without whom this battle might have been lost! Please come forward."

Parasite looked taken aback. He shook his head. "Parasite, please," Katana said with a friendly roll of her eyes.

As Beast Boy led a "Par-a-site!" chant, the janitor, still bandaged, made his way to the stage, making an effort not to make eye contact with Police Commissioner Gordon, who was striding toward him looking serious.

"Parasite," Commissioner Gordon said, stopping him. The janitor looked defeated as he held out his hands for the handcuffs. Commissioner Gordon reached for his hand . . . and shook it—but quickly, so as not to have his energy drained. "Metropolis and the world thank you for the role you played in defeating Dragon King!"

Parasite looked up, stunned. "I'm not going back to prison?"

"Not only are you not going back," he said, "but you

are getting an honorary commendation from the City of Metropolis!"

Parasite looked at Principal Waller, who added, "You've earned an extra week of vacation, but I'll expect you back here when that's up."

"Everyone," Katana yelled above the cheers, "I encourage you all to honor and respect those who have paved the way for you to become super heroes, super friends, and super citizens of the world!"

"This is *great*!" Harley yelled as she caught it all on video. "It's gonna make one heck of a special!"

Though Katana was smiling, her heart was at once full and empty. "Onna," she whispered. "Thank you. For everything."

At that moment, Katana's sword glowed once more.

EPILOGUE

As the assembly concluded and the Supers headed back to class, Miss Martian ran up to Katana and said, "You know that wooden puzzle box you made in Ms. Moone's class? The one you gave to me?"

Katana wasn't sure what she was talking about at first. That had been so long ago. Then she remembered.

"Well," Miss Martian said, looking pleased, "I finally figured it out and opened it! And guess what was inside?"

Katana gave her a *Well, tell me* shrug.

"This!" Miss Martian replied, holding something small in her hand.

Katana looked at it. It was a tiny carving of a conch shell. Had she made that? She must have, but it was so weird that she hadn't been aware of what she was doing.

"I know," Miss Martian said, almost seeming like she was reading her mind. Katana trusted Miss Martian wouldn't casually do anything like that—and she had to admit it really was a pretty obvious observation, at this point. Her friend continued. "But perhaps you did know in your heart that the conch shell would mean something very important to you one day. And it did."

She pressed the wooden shell into the palm of Katana's hand.

"I'm giving this back to you." Miss Martian grinned. "But I'm keeping the box!"

Just then a group of girls joined them. Everyone was in a great mood. It was usually like that after Hero of the Month assemblies, especially when one of their own was honored. There was much chatter and laughter, and congratulating Katana, when all heard Harley joking around.

"Help!" Harley was saying. "Someone help me!"

"She's such a crack-up," Supergirl said.

"Help!" they could hear Harley still saying. But as they turned the corner, Harley was nowhere to be seen. Instead, her ever-present video camera was on the ground.

Batgirl ran to pick it up. She looked at the video screen. On it was Harley yelling, "Help! Someone help me!" as the scene played over and over again.

"She's seriously in trouble!" Batgirl cried out.

"Wait!" said Supergirl. "Look."

Everyone crammed around the small video screen on

the camera. Harley was smiling again. "Gotcha!" she said, laughing. "I'm okay, it was all just a—"

Then a menacing shadow came up behind her—

Suddenly the screen went dark.

Mieke Kramer

Lisa Yee's debut novel, *Millicent Min, Girl Genius*, won the prestigious Sid Fleischman Humor Award. With nearly two million books in print, her other novels for young readers include *Stanford Wong Flunks Big-Time; Absolutely Maybe; Bobby vs. Girls (Accidentally); Bobby the Brave (Sometimes); Warp Speed; The Kidney Hypothetical: Or How to Ruin Your Life in Seven Days;* and American Girl's Kanani books, *Good Luck, Ivy*, and the 2016 Girl of the Year books. Lisa has been a Thurber House Children's Writer-in-Residence, and her books have been named an NPR Best Summer Read, a *Sports Illustrated Kids* Hot Summer Read, and a *USA Today* Critics' Pick, among other accolades. Visit Lisa at LisaYee.com.

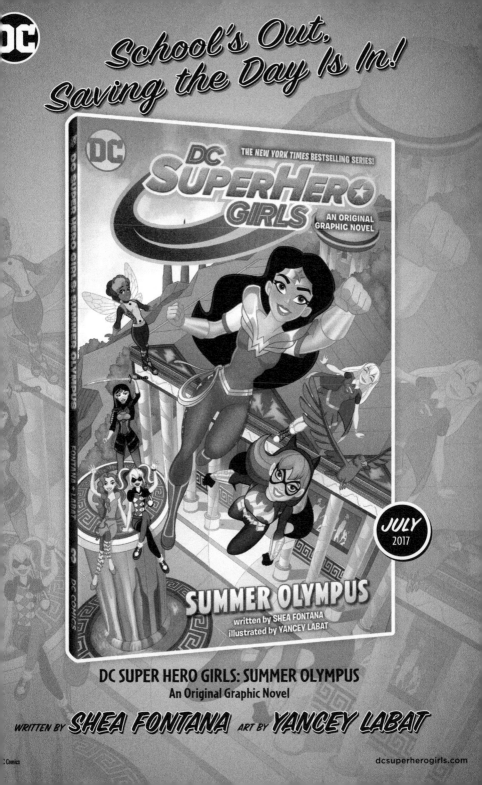